PRAISE FOR CHA

AN UNEQUAL DEFENSE

"In Zunker's solid sequel to 2019's *An Equal Justice*, Zunker . . . sustains a disciplined focus on plot and character. John Grisham fans will appreciate this familiar but effective tale."

—*Publishers Weekly*

AN EQUAL JUSTICE

"A thriller with a message. A pleasure to read. Twists I didn't see coming. I read it in one sitting."

—Robert Dugoni, #1 Amazon bestselling author of *My Sister's Grave*

"Taut, suspenseful, and action-packed with a hero you can root for, Zunker has hit it out of the park with this one."

—Victor Methos, bestselling author of *The Neon Lawyer*

"A gripping thriller with a heart, *An Equal Justice* hits the ground running . . . The chapters flew by, with surprises aplenty and taut writing. A highly recommended read that introduces a lawyer with legs."

—*Crime Thriller Hound*

"A deftly crafted legal thriller of a novel by an author with a genuine knack for a reader engaging narrative storytelling style . . ."

—Midwest Book Review

"In *An Equal Justice*, author Chad Zunker crafts a riveting legal thriller . . . *An Equal Justice* not only plunges readers into murder and conspiracy involving wealthy power players, but also immerses us in the crisis of homelessness in our country."

—*The Big Thrill*

THE TRACKER

"A gritty, compelling, and altogether engrossing novel that reads as if ripped from the headlines. I couldn't turn the pages fast enough. Chad Zunker is the real deal."

—Christopher Reich, *New York Times* bestselling author of *Numbered Account* and *Rules of Deception*

"*Good Will Hunting* meets *The Bourne Identity*."

—Fred Burton, *New York Times* bestselling author of *Under Fire*

RUNAWAY
JUSTICE

RUNAWAY JUSTICE

CHAD ZUNKER

THOMAS & MERCER

Text copyright © 2021 by Chad Zunker
All rights reserved.

Published by Thomas & Mercer, Seattle

www.apub.com

Amazon, the Amazon logo, and Thomas & Mercer are trademarks of Amazon.com, Inc., or its affiliates.

ISBN-13: 9781542025522
ISBN-10: 1542025524

Cover design by Kirk DouPonce, Dog-Eared Design

Printed in the United States of America

To Mark, Alex, and Chris,
Four Horsemen forever.

ONE

Twelve-year-old Parker Barnes could barely see five steps in front of him. But that didn't stop him from running down the narrow dirt path as fast as his skinny legs would carry him. Had he lost the guy? He wasn't sure. He couldn't hear anything except his own heartbeat pounding away in his ears. The woods were so dark that tiny tree branches kept appearing out of nowhere and smacking him in the face. He put both hands up to block the assault, but that only made him momentarily lose his balance. When the toe of his right shoe caught a sharp rock, he tumbled face-first into the dirt.

Parker pushed himself up, adjusted his black backpack, and paused to listen. He was uncertain how far he'd run. A hundred yards? Two hundred? Even though it was a cool night, his ratty gray T-shirt and blue jeans were soaked in sweat. After touching a stinging place on his left cheek, Parker held up his finger in the spotty moonlight to examine it. The liquid wasn't clear like sweat beads. It looked black—which meant he was bleeding. He could now taste the blood leaking into the corner of his mouth and wiped it away with a thumb. The blood didn't bother him too much. He'd bled a lot the last couple of years. Mostly the result of fistfights with other boys at school, which usually got him suspended a few days. That had sometimes led to more bleeding at the hands of angry foster parents.

Since his father had died three years ago, Parker had been in and out of four foster homes. Three of them were complete nightmares. He'd known only two other boys who'd been bounced around that much in such a short time. But they were both troublemakers who usually brought problems onto themselves. Parker never went looking for trouble. Yet it seemed to always be searching for him. Like tonight.

Staying perfectly still, Parker continued to listen and frantically searched the woods behind him for any sign of the man. He wondered if he should stay put or keep moving. He was willing to sit there in the dirt for hours—or until daylight—if that's what it took to get away from this guy. The goateed man wore a denim jacket over a white T-shirt and looked mean as hell.

In many ways, the guy reminded him of his last foster dad. Mr. Reid was an angry drunk. He never smiled. Never said much. He just sat in his beat-up recliner surrounded by empty beer bottles with his eyes stuck to the TV all day. Mr. Reid had lost his construction job right after Parker had moved in with them, and he was really pissed off about it. Mr. Reid's calloused hands had felt like they were covered in broken glass when they began slapping Parker around for no good reason. Then came the death threats if Parker ever told Mrs. Reid what had busted up his face real good. So Parker always lied. He knew better than to ever say anything to anyone. Telling the truth only brought more pain. He'd learned that the hard way.

But Parker hadn't been beaten in a month. When Mr. Reid had hinted at transitioning into something more sexually violent, Parker had stolen a hundred bucks out of the empty coffee container Mrs. Reid had hidden on the top shelf of the pantry and had bolted from the home in the middle of the night. No way in hell was he going to wait around for Mr. Reid's next drunken episode. Five miles up the road, he'd stowed away in the back of a dirty horse trailer at a truck stop gas station. He'd then logged probably two hundred miles while sitting in a stall filled with horse crap before he'd finally jumped out at a stoplight while passing through Austin.

Although Parker had never been to the city, his dad had always loved the Texas Longhorns. He'd taught Parker how to do the "hook 'em" hand sign as a toddler and had promised to take him to a football game one day. That didn't happen—and now, of course, it never would. But Austin seemed like a good place to set up his new life. He was for sure never going back to that damn foster home—or *any* foster home, for that matter. He'd rather take his chances out on the streets. He'd heard a story once at the boys' home about another kid his age who'd chosen the same runaway path and had survived just fine. Parker knew he was every bit as tough as that kid. At least that's what he kept telling himself. He didn't feel so tough tonight.

The sound of a branch breaking on the trail somewhere behind him sent a sharp chill straight up his sweaty back. Parker held his breath as his eyes narrowed. Then he noticed a shadow of movement twenty paces away, followed by a splash of moonlight across the man's hard face. Parker cursed, scrambled to his feet, and took off again.

"Come on, boy!" the man called out. "Stop running—I just want to talk!"

Parker knew that was a lie. The man had a gun. And not just any gun—a gun with one of those longer barrels that kind of muffled the shot. Parker had just seen him use it. He felt like he was watching a scene from one of those John Wick films. It looked cool in the movies but not in real life. There was no way he was stopping to talk to this guy about *anything*.

Darting around more trees, Parker spotted light up ahead. It looked like the dirt trail spilled out into a parking lot next to a strip of buildings. The return of the city. If he could somehow get there, Parker could easily get himself lost again. After a month out on the streets, he knew how to hide like a cockroach in the cracks of this town.

His legs propelled him forward even faster. If his worn tennis shoes hadn't been filled with so many holes in the toes, he'd have probably gotten away from this dude already. His feet hadn't seen new shoes since he was ten and had lived with the Bidwell family for a couple of months. They were good people with money who had taken him shopping several times with their son, Judd, who was a year older than Parker. He'd really liked Judd. They used to play basketball for hours every day in the driveway. But then Mrs. Bidwell suddenly got cancer—just like Parker's mom had when he was seven—and she went downhill fast. The home went from happy to sad overnight.

Shortly thereafter, Parker had gotten picked up by someone from the system and taken back to the boys' home. That day had sucked big-time. He'd never forget watching Judd wave goodbye from the driveway. The next day, Parker had gotten beaten up by two older bullies at the boys' home who stole his brand-new basketball shoes. He'd tried to tell the director what had happened, but she wouldn't listen. Adults *never* did. Then he'd gotten a second beatdown for ratting on the boys.

Story of his life—at least since his dad had died.

But things had been better on his own the past month. Parker was scrappy. He was finding food here and there okay. By following the street crowd, he'd figured out where Austin fed its poor and homeless on any given day. He was a scrawny kid and didn't need much to survive anyway. There was a group of older teenage runaways like him who hung out near the main drag by the UT campus. Parker stayed around the fringes of that group. A few of them had been looking out for him. He'd learned to live each day in the shadows, where adults wouldn't notice him and begin to wonder why a kid his age was out on the streets all by himself. He didn't want any adults trying to *help* him. He would never trust an adult again.

Parker was five feet from the clearing into the parking lot when he heard the muffled sound of the gun suddenly explode behind him—the same sound he'd heard just a few minutes ago—and then he felt his backpack jerk him sideways, like someone had grabbed it and yanked him hard to the right. He fell forward, tumbled to the dirt again, and then rolled out onto the hard pavement of the parking lot.

For a moment, he wondered if he'd been shot. He didn't feel anything. Had the bullet only hit his backpack? In the movies, a guy would sometimes get shot and not even realize it until he'd finally stopped running or fighting. Then the dude would find the bullet wound and usually die while sitting there bleeding out. Was that what would happen to him? Parker immediately got to his feet again, peered over to his left at a gas station. There were several cars parked at the pumps with people standing around, waiting. Had anyone heard the gunshot? Did they think it was a random city noise? They all just continued to stare mindlessly at their phones.

Parker raced forward, hoping the man behind him wasn't willing to shoot at him in the wide-open parking lot. He zigged and zagged, just in case, thinking it might make the guy miss. He was now fully exposed under a security light as he approached the building. He felt completely vulnerable, which only made him run faster. His lungs were on fire, but he knew he couldn't stop. Those waiting at the gas pumps turned to stare at him as he rushed past. Parker thought of running up to one of them and screaming for help but decided against it. The guy might shoot him if he stopped running. Instead, he crossed into the city street in front of the gas station, where he just barely evaded a metro bus that had unexpectedly pulled around the corner. The bus screeched to a stop. Several horns honked, and more brakes squealed from other cars evading a wreck.

Parker hurried up to another strip of buildings, followed a sidewalk at full speed, not even slowing enough to peek behind him. He didn't stop running for what felt like a mile, until his legs gave out on him. Finally, he collapsed in a dirty alley, where he pushed himself up against the protection of a dumpster and gasped for breath. He took off the backpack and found the large hole in the side of it. This made his eyes go wide. He then examined himself all over. He spotted a gob of blood on the front of his T-shirt, but it wasn't his blood. It looked like he'd survived the encounter with no injuries other than some bad scratches on his face.

Sitting there, Parker wondered what he should do next. Should he go to the police? Tell them what he saw? He shook his head. No way. The cops never believed kids—at least, not kids like him. He was better off keeping his mouth shut. He leaned his head back against the dumpster and gradually caught his breath again. He was so tired. He felt like he could sleep for a week straight. He probably could if he'd had a real bed. He hated that part of life on the streets. Sleeping on concrete, on benches, and even on top of picnic tables—like he had been doing tonight in the park before two cars had unexpectedly arrived and startled him awake.

Closing his eyes, Parker was sure he would drift off right away. But then his mind began reliving every second of the brutal scene he'd just witnessed, and his eyes immediately popped back open. He put his hand to his chest and could feel his heart racing wildly again. When he started to tremble all over, Parker wrapped his arms around his legs, pulled them in real close, and held himself in the tightest ball possible.

Burying his face into his knees, he began to quietly cry.

TWO

Four days later

David Adams kicked his bare feet up onto the wooden balcony railing of his newly rented garage apartment and sipped from a cold bottle of Dos Equis. The apartment was nestled on top of a small hill in an old neighborhood just a few blocks south of downtown Austin. David had made it a nightly ritual to sit in this perch and watch the city lights sparkle and dance across the calm water of the Colorado River. It helped him clear his head of whatever craziness he'd encountered that day as a lawyer to a growing number of misfit clients.

Today's episode had involved a homeless man named Cletus, who kept quietly chanting magic spells at the judge during his hearing on a drunk and disorderly charge. Cletus was harmless, even though he had a raggedy red beard that nearly touched his belly button and was known to howl at the moon while camping under the interstate. David knew decades of sleeping on hard concrete could really warp someone's mind. It was only David's credibility with the judge that had gotten his client a small fine and probation. Cletus had then pulled fifteen wrinkled bucks out of his pocket and handed them to David, which was more than what many of his street friends usually paid him. Fortunately, David had rounded up a few more legitimate clients recently that helped him make ends meet.

He'd begun renting the unattached garage apartment six months ago when an unexpected windfall of cash from a client had allowed him to move off the crappy backroom sofa at his office. The narrow balcony had room for only one plastic patio chair. The living space inside barely held much more than that. A sleeper sofa. A dresser. A rolltop desk. A beanbag chair. A small TV. A bar table next to a kitchenette. All items he'd collected at garage sales.

An eightysomething widow named Mrs. Bishop with a globe of bright-white hair owned the property and lived in the yellow two-story Victorian twenty feet away. David had helped her grandson get probation and go into rehab after he'd been arrested for stealing a motorcycle. Mrs. Bishop would often wake him before dawn and ask him to do odd jobs around her house. David didn't mind too much, considering rent was dirt cheap, and he could easily walk to his office across the Congress Avenue Bridge.

Touching the bottle to his lips, David allowed his eyes to drift across the tall buildings of the downtown skyline. They settled for a moment on the glorious Frost Bank Tower, his first legal home after graduating with honors from Stanford Law. Just about a year ago, David was making more money than he'd ever dreamed as a first-year associate at the most prestigious law firm in town, being profiled in local magazines while living in a fancy high-rise condo and driving an expensive SUV. But his life had spiraled out of control there in more ways than one. So he chose to walk away in order to better serve the city's most vulnerable outcasts.

Although he never missed the legal work, he certainly missed the perks.

When his cell phone buzzed, David pulled it from his pocket and stared at the screen. Skater was calling him. David had met the teenage drifter six months ago when he was defending a client who'd been framed on murder charges as part of a dark political conspiracy. Since then, David had helped Skater here and there when the kid got into a bit of trouble with the police—which seemed to be happening more often lately.

David answered. "It's late, Skater. What do you want?"

"Sorry, Shep. But I really need your help."

Most of David's homeless friends called him Shep, a nickname given to him by a street preacher named Benny last year because he'd said David had the same name as King David, the great shepherd in the Bible.

"Yeah, I didn't figure you were calling to chitchat."

"It ain't me this time, I swear. See, this is about someone else."

"Who?"

"Kid named Parker. Cops just picked him up."

"Why?"

"Well, see, we was, uh, you know, trying to make some cash."

"What the hell did you do, Skater?"

"We was, uh, grabbing purses," Skater admitted.

David sighed. "You told me you were done with that."

"I was. I am. I dunno, Shep. We get hungry out here. And this seemed easy. Plus, the kid was *really* good at it. He's so small, he goes unnoticed."

"So good that he got himself busted?"

"Yeah, well, see, that was my fault. I was stupid and got greedy."

"You keep calling him a kid. Why? You're just a kid."

Skater was maybe seventeen. But he'd been out on the streets by himself for several years already.

"Nah, man, Parker's like a *real* kid. See, he's only like twelve, I think."

"What? You pulled a twelve-year-old boy into one of your schemes?"

"I already said I was stupid, okay?"

"Where are the boy's parents?"

9

"Ain't got none. He's a runaway, like me. Will you help?"

David rubbed his face with his free hand. "Where did he get picked up?"

"We was working over by the food trailers on Barton Springs."

"Does Parker have a last name?"

"Probably. But I don't know it."

"All right, fine, I'll check in on him."

"Thanks, Shep! You're the best! I swear on my momma's grave, this is the last time . . ."

"Yeah, yeah. Stay out of trouble."

David hung up without listening to the rest of Skater's grandiose oath. He'd heard it several times already. Not that he held it against the teenager. The kid had experienced things that most people couldn't fathom. Mom had been a meth addict in El Paso who'd kept trying to pimp her own son out to her druggie boyfriends. Then she'd overdosed, and a ruthless dealer had tried to lock Skater in a closet for his own business. Skater had managed to claw his way out through the Sheetrock before something worse happened. He'd hit the road at fourteen and never looked back. Even though the kid drove him crazy, David empathized. Being constantly despised and ignored had left most of David's street friends in a state of perpetual hopelessness and despair. So they did what they had to do at times to survive the day.

Which kept David very busy as a lawyer.

THREE

David parked his beat-up fifteen-year-old Chevy truck along the curb in front of the Gardener Betts Juvenile Justice Center, a complex of several brick buildings off South Congress Avenue where the city's juvenile delinquents were held, processed, and jailed, if necessary. Wearing jeans and a blue sweatshirt hoodie, he trotted up the sidewalk to the Meurer Intermediate Sanctions Center and pushed through glass doors to a security checkpoint staffed by two imposing deputies. The lobby was mostly empty since it was after normal visiting hours. David passed through the security scanner and then found a bored-looking young deputy with bright-red hair staring at a computer screen behind a front counter.

"I need to visit with a potential client," David said, flashing his ID and signing in on a clipboard.

"Name?" the guy asked, eyes still on his computer.

"Parker something."

The guy looked up at him with a wrinkled brow.

"I don't know his last name yet, okay?" David explained. "But the kid was brought in about thirty minutes ago, so he should be easy to find. Petty theft, I think. Supposed to be around twelve years old."

The guy typed on the keyboard. "Yep, Parker Barnes. Purse snatcher."

"Great. I need to see Mr. Barnes."

"All right. Gimme a minute. I'll have him brought over to Room 4."

David followed a hallway lined with empty visitation rooms and entered Room 4. Small and clean with a square table and two chairs, the room had a big glass window looking out toward the hallway. David had been inside this building only once before when dealing with another juvenile situation. The facility was a step up from the grime and grit of the regular county jail—these were still kids, after all—but it was still very much on lockdown. He waited ten minutes before a deputy arrived at the door with the scrawniest twelve-year-old boy David had ever seen. Parker had shaggy brown hair that hung to his shoulders and covered half of his gaunt face. The orange juvie jumpsuit looked three sizes too big for him. There were a few scrapes and bruises on his face. Parker kept his eyes mostly on the floor as the deputy guided him inside the room.

"Can you at least get him a uniform that fits?" David asked the deputy.

The deputy frowned. "Come on, man. You get what you get. This ain't a day spa, you know."

The deputy shut the door behind him and left David alone with Parker, who just stood there with his shoulders sagging.

"Hey, Parker, my name's David Adams. I'm an attorney."

Parker glanced up at him. He had the bluest eyes David had ever seen. But they were near slits right now as he glared hard at David.

"So what," he muttered.

"You doing okay?" David asked.

An eye roll. "Yeah, sure, I'm just great. What do you think?"

For a small kid, he had a big attitude.

"Right. Can we sit down and talk for a second?"

"Do I have a choice?"

"Yes, you do."

A slight shrug. "Whatever."

David sat in one of the chairs, crossed his hands on the table in front of him. Parker found his way to the other chair and sank down into it. He sat so low in his seat that David could barely see the kid's eyes over the tabletop.

"I don't have any money, mister," Parker said. "I can't pay for a lawyer."

"I'm not asking for money."

Parker's face bunched up. "Why? My dad always said lawyers don't do a damn thing without charging you an arm and a leg for it first."

"Where is your dad?"

"He's dead. Where's yours?"

"Also dead," David calmly replied. "What about your mom?"

"She's dead, too. Thanks for bringing it up."

"I'm real sorry. Brothers or sisters? Aunts? Uncles? Grandparents?"

"Nope. No one. All on my own. Life sucks, right?"

"Sometimes," David agreed. "Look, Skater called me about twenty minutes ago. That's why I'm here. He asked me to help you."

Parker looked up at him. "He get away?"

"Yeah, I guess so."

"Cool," Parker said with a small grin.

"He feels bad about what happened to you tonight. Says it was his fault."

"Nah, Skater didn't make me do anything."

"I'll tell him you said that. Are you a runaway, Parker?"

Parker shrugged but didn't answer him. Instead, he said, "The last lawyer who offered to help me and my dad screwed us over big-time. My dad hired him to go after the insurance company after my mom died. They wouldn't pay up like they were supposed to do. So we lawyered up and hired some slick con artist. That stupid lawyer made all these promises about getting us our insurance money if we paid up front. But he never made good. And then he stopped answering my dad's phone calls. I'd never seen my dad so pissed. I remember one day in particular he threw his phone against the kitchen wall and shattered it into, like, a thousand pieces."

"Then it makes sense why you wouldn't trust lawyers."

"Yeah. But I don't trust anyone."

David studied the kid. He had an innocent face, but there was definitely a hard edge to him. Losing both parents at a young age could do that to someone. David remembered the feeling well; he'd lost his own father as a child and then his mother as a teenager. After his mother had died, he was so angry, he wanted to burn the whole world down and take everyone with him. He started doing drugs and even stole a car one night. He was well on his way to sitting in a juvie center, just like Parker was right now, when his older sister, Brandy, moved home from college and kicked his ass around until he got his life back on track. It worked. From there, he'd gone on to college at Abilene Christian University and then off to law school. He owed everything he was today to his sister. But Parker didn't have a big sister to rescue him.

"If you don't mind me asking, Parker, how did your mom die?"

"Cancer. Her ovaries or something."

"How old were you?"

"Seven. Feels like forever ago."

"What about your dad? What happened to him?"

Parker swallowed, stared at his hands. This one seemed to hit him even harder. "He was late picking me up from soccer practice. He was always running late after my mom died, and I kept whining to him about how much it sucked always being the last kid picked up. So I guess he was driving really fast that day, trying to not upset me again. Cops said he lost control of our car and rammed it straight into a tree. So, you know, he's basically dead because of me."

"Come on, Parker. That's not being fair to yourself."

But David understood why the boy felt that way. He'd blamed himself for years for his mother's sudden death. She'd exhausted herself, working three jobs at times so he could go to the best football camps and have all the latest sports gear. David had only started letting go of that guilt over this past year.

"Nothing in life is fair, Mr. Adams. You're a lawyer; you should know that. Cops told me my dad was dead on impact. Probably a lie. Adults always lie about that kind of stuff, thinking they're protecting kids."

"My dad also died in a car wreck. I was six."

Parker looked up at him with a wrinkled brow. "For real?"

David nodded. "I lost my mom when I was sixteen. She had a heart attack. Here one day and gone the next."

"Are you lying?" Parker asked with narrowed eyes. "Because therapists are always doing that kind of thing. Making stuff up because they think if they can somehow connect with us on the pain, we will suddenly start sharing about our whole lives or something. It never worked with me."

"No, I'm not lying. Just saying I know how much life can suck."

Parker sat up straighter, put his hands on the table. "No offense, Mr. Adams, but how is us sitting here talking about our dead parents going to help me? They had nothing to do with this. I'm just some stupid street kid who got busted. There's really not much more to it than that."

"First of all, you're clearly *not* stupid." The boy talked more eloquently than most of his adult clients. "And if I'm going to help get you out of here, I need to know some of your background."

"You can get me out of here?"

"Maybe. You ever been arrested before?"

"Nope."

"How long have you been living out on the streets?"

Parker shrugged his bony shoulders. "About a month. And I'm doing just fine on my own."

"Wearing that orange jumpsuit suggests otherwise. Where were you living before hitting the streets?"

"With foster parents. But I'm never going back there."

"Well, the judge might have something to say about that. Running away from home is a status offense."

"A status offense? What's that mean?"

"It means it's a crime because you're a kid."

Parker's eyes widened. "You mean the judge can make me go back?"

"Sure. If the judge thinks that's the best thing for you."

A wave of panic suddenly spread across the boy's entire face. "You can't let the judge do that to me, Mr. Adams. Please don't let them send me back to that place. I'll go anywhere else."

"Why, Parker? Was someone hurting you?"

Parker didn't respond, but his eyes said everything.

"Your foster dad?" David asked.

The boy's eyes immediately grew wet.

David felt anger rise up in his chest. "You tell your caseworker?"

Parker shook his head and said, his voice cracking, "Would you tell if someone had threatened to peel your skin right off your own body?"

David cursed, then apologized for his language.

"I'll run away again," Parker continued, growing more emotional by the second. "You tell the judge if they try to send me back there, I'll just keep running away. Or worse. Maybe I'll try to kill Mr. Reid. Tell the judge that, Mr. Adams. Then his blood will be on the judge's hands."

"Okay, calm down. I get it. Stop talking that way. Especially don't say anything like that in front of the judge tomorrow. Believe me—that's not going to help us. I'll work on another solution. Okay?"

Parker nodded and exhaled, but David could see his fingers still shaking.

"In the meantime, just keep to yourself in here," David urged him. "Don't mess with anyone or get into any other trouble. I'll be back first thing in the morning for the hearing."

David stood to get the deputy out in the hallway.

"Mr. Adams?"

David turned back around to look at the boy.

"Thanks for coming tonight," Parker said. "I mean it."

David swallowed. The tough lines that had been so prevalent in the kid's face when he'd entered the room a few minutes ago had completely disappeared. All David could see now was a scared and desperate little boy who was pleading for rescue. David wanted to scoop Parker up right then and there, take him home, and make sure nothing ever happened to him again. The kid needed a break in the worst way possible.

"Everything will be okay," David reassured him. "Trust me."

FOUR

David had a tough time sleeping that night while thinking about Parker's tragic story and the kid having to stay over at the juvenile facility. He just kept tossing and turning. So he got out of bed early, did a five-mile jog around Lady Bird Lake, showered, and then headed into the office well before the rest of the business crowd. His firm, Gray & Adams LLP, leased a small office suite on the second level of a run-down three-story redbrick building that sat in the heart of downtown. They'd nearly gotten evicted six months ago because the building's new owner wasn't too fond of David's homeless clients hanging around. But a wave of good publicity following a big case and an influx of unexpected cash had allowed them to fight the eviction and work out a new lease agreement.

The office didn't have fancy rugs or expensive artwork—or any artwork for that matter—but it was home. David's personal office looked out over Congress Avenue. If he peered far enough to his left, David could see the pink granite of the Texas Capitol building. His partner, Thomas Gray, had the office next door to his. A small entryway held a circular table and acted as their conference room. A third back room was used as the firm's library, storage, and kitchen. They'd recently added an additional office next door. David had set up three computer stations in the new space where his clients could go online to check on potential jobs, manage their healthcare benefits, set up doctors' appointments, and connect with estranged family members.

Doc came into the office around eight. A tall and slender man in his late fifties with salt-and-pepper hair, Doc was the firm's only full-time staff member. A former high school history teacher before he'd battled alcohol addiction and a long season of homelessness, Doc was a wiz at research and had quickly become a valuable asset to the firm. David had first met Doc a year ago when Benny the street preacher had walked David deep into the woods to visit the Camp—a secret tent community for a group of homeless men. Doc had been one of the founders before it had tragically burned to the ground. The men who'd lived at the Camp had scattered around the city while trying to find new places to sleep and survive. Most of them had struggled. The strength and support they'd all found in the community of the Camp had been fractured.

But David had been working hard to resolve that for them. Benny had dreamed of creating a legitimate village for his homeless friends with micro-homes, bathhouses, and even a building with a commercial-grade kitchen, where the boys could share meals, throw parties, and host church services. Before David had left his high-paying gig over at Hunter & Kellerman, he'd managed to purchase a plot of twenty acres in East Austin in hopes of carrying Benny's dream forward. Four months ago he'd connected with the founder of a local homeless non-profit who'd shared the same unique vision. They'd quickly formed a partnership to move things forward, and David had donated the land. Gray & Adams LLP then made a significant financial investment. With other financial backers coming on board, Benny's Village was now in full-on development. Fifteen micro-homes were currently being built, with more planned. The first residents—which included most of the boys from the Camp—would be moving into their brand-new homes by the end of the month. Benny's great sacrifice had paid off in a profound way.

David looked up from his desk when Doc walked into his office and handed him a set of papers.

"The kid's file from CPS," Doc said. "They just sent it over."

"Thanks, Doc."

"That kid has been through hell, huh?"

"Yeah, it's brutal. Way too much pain for his brief life."

"I hate to see that. You need anything else?"

"I'm good for now. Thanks."

David began to scan Parker's official file. Parker Eugene Barnes. Born in Houston twelve years ago to Todd and Trisha Barnes. Both deceased. Entered the foster care system three years ago. In and out of four homes. Removed from the first home because of physical abuse. There were a couple of color photos on the page. A nine-year-old Parker had a black eye and a heavily bruised right arm. David shook his head. He then read a summary about Parker's removal from the home of Michael and Allison Bidwell after Mrs. Bidwell had been diagnosed with cancer. Another mention of foster parents who'd been arrested for dealing drugs while Parker and two other kids were living with them. David scanned the report to find the names of his latest foster parents. Mack and Leslie Reid. There was nothing in the report mentioning any type of abuse situation with the Reids. Of course, Parker had said he'd never told anyone.

Jumping on his laptop, David did a quick search for Mack Reid in Wallis, Texas. There were a few mentions of the name but nothing prominent. But there was one photo from the *Wallis News-Review* showing men from a softball team holding up a trophy. Mack Reid stood in the middle. The guy had a thick beard and must've been six-five and 250 pounds. The thought of this giant man striking a kid like Parker made David livid. What kind of loser did something like that?

David looked up when he heard a ruckus coming from the hallway. A lady yelling at someone? What the hell? David jumped up from his chair, hurried through the entry room, and opened the door to the hallway. Right outside his door, he found an attractive woman in her midtwenties with long black hair, dressed in all black—black leather jacket, black slacks, black heels—standing there and berating Bobby E. Lee, who was the firm's unofficial security guard. A homeless black man in his seventies with a prominent white beard, Bobby Lee wore the same gray Confederate soldier uniform every day and sat in a chair outside the firm's office door like he was guarding a military fort. Every time David entered and exited the office, Bobby Lee would stand and salute him like a loyal soldier. The odd behavior just came with the territory as David interacted with the homeless community day in and day out.

"What's going on out here?" David asked, looking back and forth between the woman and Bobby Lee, who seemed shocked at the altercation.

"I'll tell you what," the woman snapped. "This dude here just tried to steal my purse. He's lucky I didn't break his damn arm."

David looked over at his office guard. "Bobby?"

"No, sir, Mr. Adams. I swear. The purse dropped off her shoulder, and I was only reaching down to get it for her. I wasn't trying to steal nothing."

David glanced back at the woman with a head tilt.

She frowned. "What? You're going to believe some weird guy in a costume who probably shouldn't even be inside this building?"

"Bobby is my friend," David clarified. "And someone I trust."

"Oh, well, fine. But I don't want him touching my purse again."

"You've made that very clear," David said, annoyed. "Can I help you with something?"

"Actually, I'm here to help you. You're David Adams?"

"Who are you?"

"Jess Raven, special investigator."

21

She stuck out her hand. He hesitantly shook it.

"You're Jess Raven?"

"Why do you look so surprised?"

David had received an email yesterday from Judge Laymon Martin with a note saying help was coming his way along with an attached court-appointed document assigning Jessica Michelle Raven to forty hours of pro bono investigative work at his firm. David had a cordial relationship with Judge Martin, who always seemed supportive of his efforts to provide legal assistance to the city's underprivileged community. So the judge would send people David's way here and there to help out around the firm as part of their probationary terms. Something David really appreciated since they were understaffed. When David had gotten the email from the judge yesterday, he'd pictured a tough older woman with short gray hair who'd maybe been a detective or something. Not someone who looked like the woman in front of him.

"You're just, uh, not what I expected," he said.

"Sorry to disappoint," Jess replied. "But, hey, if you want to go ahead and sign off on my hours for the judge, I'll gladly walk out right now and leave you and your purse-snatching best friend here alone."

David grinned. "Well, I'd hate to disrespect Judge Martin's request in that way."

David led Jess inside the entry room of the office suite, shut the door behind them. "Welcome to Gray and Adams."

She gave a quick look around. "Wow, this place is a real dump. No wonder you don't have any office photos posted online."

"Do you always say whatever is on your mind?"

She flashed a quick smile. "Yes, it's part of my charm. You'll grow to appreciate it."

"We'll see. So what did you do to get probation?"

A small shrug. "Put someone in their place, that's all."

"Come on. Give me the juicy details."

"Fine. Do you know Edward Rossali?"

"I know of him."

Edward Rossali was the senior partner at Rossali, Meekins & Tobian, one of the bigger corporate litigation firms in town. David's old firm, Hunter & Kellerman, used to battle them all the time for big-money clients.

"I was an investigator over there for the past year."

"Was?" David asked.

"Well, things changed after I cracked three of Rossali's ribs with a punch and then shattered the tibia bone in his right leg with a kick."

"Ouch. Why'd you do that?"

"Sleazeball was under the impression he was paying for more than just my investigative abilities. He grabbed my ass, and I worked him over good."

"Three broken ribs and a broken leg?"

She shrugged. "I might've gotten carried away. But believe me—he deserved it. He was always harassing other female staff members. I can't tell you how many hidden smiles I got from the staff while I was being escorted out of there in handcuffs. I was more hero than criminal that day."

"So he pressed charges?"

"Of course. He straight up lied to the police and told them I assaulted him when he confronted me about stealing property from the firm. So I spent the night in lockup."

"Damn. What a jerk."

"No big deal. I look good in that gray-striped jumpsuit."

"But Judge Martin only gave you probation?"

"Yeah, I don't think the judge was buying too much of Rossali's concocted story about me being a master laptop thief. But I guess he couldn't simply let me walk out of his courtroom scot-free after I'd put the guy in the hospital. So here I am, at your service. Just keep your hands to yourself, and we should be fine."

"Good advice."

"So what kind of law firm is this, anyway? Your crappy one-page website doesn't say too much. By the looks of this office, I'm guessing you mostly represent pawnshops, drug dealers, and pimps."

David laughed. "Not quite. My partner handles family law and adoption matters. He's at a law conference in Chicago this week, so I doubt you'll meet him. My primary focus is on street clients, although I operate all over the map doing general litigation."

She pitched her head as if something had just dawned on her. "Wait a second? Are you that lawyer I read about a few months ago who represented the homeless guy in that case with the dead prosecutor?"

"Yes, that's me."

Jess rolled her eyes. "Of course."

"Is there a problem?"

"I'm just not much of a fan, that's all."

"Of me? Or of my clients?"

"The latter. I haven't decided about you just yet."

"Fair enough. What's your hang-up with the homeless?"

"It's just . . . nothing. Bad experiences, that's all."

Jess didn't expound, and David didn't push her on it. "So, what's your background? How'd you become an investigator?"

"Do I have to interview for this free gig?"

"No, I just like to know who I'm working with."

"Good. Because my reference list really sucks at the moment. All right, let's see. Dad was a police officer. Mom worked in crime scene forensics for a while. After serving in the navy, I joined the Naval Criminal Investigative Service in Washington. NCIS, like the TV show. Then Mom got really sick last year, so I moved back to Austin to help take care of her. My boss in DC knew a couple of bigwig lawyers here in town, said I could make twice the money doing investigative work for these corporate law firms. Mom's healthcare costs were skyrocketing, so I took the gig. Things were actually going pretty well until Rossali got handsy with me. What about you? Why'd you become a lawyer?"

"Pretty simple. I grew up dirt poor and wanted to be rich."

She took another glance around the office and scrunched up her face. "I think you took a wrong turn somewhere, buddy."

David laughed. "It's a long story. Look, I have to run over to a court hearing this morning. Can you hang, and we can talk more when I get back?"

"Sure. I'll just be here clutching my purse tightly."

FIVE

David came fully prepared to Parker's court hearing in front of the juvenile judge. First thing that morning, he'd filed an official report with CPS asserting physical abuse involving Parker's foster father Mack Reid. David was determined to see that situation all the way through to ensure the monster never got his hands on another vulnerable child. After giving the judge a copy of the CPS report and explaining why Parker had been living alone out on the streets, David had then offered an alternative housing solution at a local at-risk youth facility called Hand-Up Home. David personally knew the director there and had already made a phone call. Parker wasn't crazy about the idea but agreed to it anyway. As the kid had told him last night, he'd do anything to not go back to his foster parents. Because Parker had no other marks on his criminal record, the judge was sympathetic. David was able to get her to release him with a probationary period. The theft charge would be dropped as long as Parker stayed out of trouble.

After the hearing, David waited in the lobby until Parker was finally led out of a back room. He was no longer wearing the ridiculously oversize orange jail jumpsuit. Instead, he had on a pair of blue jeans, worn sneakers, and a black sweatshirt hoodie with superhero Iron Man on the front. The hood was already up over his head and covering his disheveled hair. He looked like a normal child. A kid who should be playing video games with friends, or soccer, or hanging out at the mall. Not a kid living on the streets, struggling to find his next meal. They exited the building and hit the sidewalk toward the parking lot across the street. Parker didn't seem to be in much of a mood for chitchat, so David just let him be for a moment. He figured going from an abusive foster situation to living on the streets for weeks, getting arrested, staying overnight in jail, and now being sent to a brand-new place was a lot for any twelve-year-old to process.

They climbed into David's old truck.

"I thought lawyers made a lot of money," Parker remarked, his eyes scanning the inside of the beat-up vehicle.

David smiled. "Some do. You hungry?"

"Starving. Food in there sucks."

"You like breakfast tacos?"

"Sure. Anything!"

"I know just the place."

David drove straight to Torchy's Tacos, where they sat in a booth inside and gorged themselves on a full order of breakfast tacos. Parker ordered three with egg, bacon, and cheese, and he ate all of them before David had even finished his first.

"The judge was nice," David remarked.

"Yeah. But do I really have to go to this place, Mr. Adams? I promise you, I can handle myself just fine out on my own. I don't need any supervision."

"You have to go, Parker," David insisted. "The judge only released you to me because I assured her that you would be in a stable situation under my direct care. If you skip out and the judge finds out, it won't go well for either of us. You'll be right back in there. So you have to promise me you'll be on good behavior and not do *anything* to make things worse."

Parker relented. "I promise."

"Plus, like I told you, I know the director at Hand-Up Home. Keith's a really good guy. You're going to like him. It won't be so bad."

"It's just, well, I've never had much luck in places like this. Older boys always pick on me because I'm smaller. I feel like I'm always walking around with a dang target on my back or something. I don't know."

"Keith won't let that happen, okay?"

Parker nodded, then eyeballed one of the tacos still sitting in David's food basket. "You going to eat that or what, Mr. Adams?"

David smiled, shoved his taco across the table. "Help yourself."

Parker did just that, ingesting it in big bites just like he had the other three. The boy ate like he hadn't seen real food in weeks.

"Hey, Parker, you like football?"

Parker looked up, still chewing. "Football?"

"Yeah, you know, touchdowns, field goals, and such."

Parker grinned. "Sure, I like football. My dad and me used to throw the ball around the backyard all the time. He always said I had a real good arm—that maybe someday I could play ball in college or something, if we kept practicing, but . . ."

David knew how that sentence ended, so he jumped back in to keep the mood light. "I played football in college."

The boy's eyes lit up. "Really?"

David nodded. "When I was your age, all I wanted to do was play in the NFL. I was pretty good, too, until my knee got busted up. So I had to quit."

"What position?"

"Quarterback."

"Cool! That's what I want to play."

"Anyway, I was thinking about getting tickets to the UT game next Saturday. The Longhorns are playing Oklahoma State. Want to go with me?"

Parker stopped chewing. "For real?"

"Yeah, sure. I'm friends with another lawyer who has season tickets. He's always offering them to me. I thought it might be fun for us . . ." David could see the boy's eyes unexpectedly begin to water. It caught him off guard. "Hey, what is it, kid?"

Parker swallowed, quickly wiped his eyes with the sleeve of his hoodie. "It's . . . nothing. I just, my dad . . . I've just never been to a real football game before. That's all."

"Well, then, let's change that."

Parker's smile grew so big, David could see every tiny bit of bacon and egg still in the cracks of his teeth.

After breakfast, David made a quick stop at a gas station to fill up his truck on the way to the Hand-Up Home. He asked Parker if he wanted any snacks. Parker went straight to the candy aisle and grabbed himself a mega-size TWIX bar.

"This is my favorite," he told David.

"Then you'd better get at least two of them."

Parker excitedly grabbed another giant TWIX bar, and then David paid at the counter. Climbing back into the truck, Parker tore open one of the candy bars and began munching on it as they made the short drive to Hand-Up Home off Thirty-Eighth Street. David parked in a small lot in front of the administration building. The facility had been created as a safe haven for children healing from physical, emotional, and sexual abuse, neglect, or abandonment. Many of the kids suffered from serious emotional disorders and needed twenty-four-hour supervision, so they wouldn't harm themselves or others. Because of this, the facility operated under tight security.

As they walked up to the main doors, David could tell that Parker was getting a bit nervous. The kid kept lagging behind. David put his hand on the boy's shoulder, trying to reassure him. Inside, David told a receptionist they were there to see Keith. The director walked out of a back hallway to greet them a few seconds later. Keith Bagley was in his midforties with graying hair and a beard and came across as one of the friendliest guys David had ever met. He'd gotten to know Keith over the past year because many of Thomas's clients were in the thick of the foster care and adoption process. Keith had been in their office on several occasions.

They shook hands. Then Keith knelt in front of Parker.

"You must be Parker."

Parker nodded but didn't say anything.

"My name's Keith. Welcome to Hand-Up."

"Thanks," Parker quietly managed.

"How about I give you a quick tour of the place?"

Parker shrugged. "Okay."

Keith led them through a series of secure doors—every new section entry required a card key—and into the main children's wing. Keith explained how forty kids currently stayed with them. Most of the rooms had bunk beds shared by boys close in age. There were classrooms along one side of the wing. Keith said that a lot of the children did their studies on-site, while a few were still bused off to various schools. They exited a glass door to a back courtyard, which had picnic tables, a basketball court, and a deluxe playground. The entire courtyard was encircled by a tall black wrought-iron fence with spiky points at the top. It wasn't exactly razor wire, but its purpose was the same—to keep flight-risk kids from running.

Keith asked Parker if he liked video games.

Another shrug. "Sure. Who doesn't?"

"Well, some of the other boys around your age are learning how to make their very own superhero video games over in our computer lab. Do you want to join them?"

That seemed to spark his interest. "Yeah, cool."

"I'll give you a minute with David and then walk you over."

Alone, David knelt down in front of Parker. "What do you think?"

"It's all right, I guess."

"Just all right? I'd love to have my own basketball court."

They shared a small grin.

"It's only temporary, okay?" David added. "Until we can find you a stable foster situation with someone I've fully vetted."

Parker nodded. "I know."

"Look, I've got to run, okay? But I'll be checking on you every day. And you have my phone number if you need anything."

"I'm good, Mr. Adams. I swear."

"Okay. Remember not to make any plans for next Saturday. We'll head over to the stadium early to get you some Longhorn gear to wear."

"I can't wait!"

SIX

After saying goodbye to Parker at the computer lab, David followed Keith back to the lobby of the main administrative building, where they stepped right into the middle of a commotion. Four imposing men were all hovering around the receptionist, who looked completely overwhelmed. Three of the guys wore the same dark-blue windbreakers. The midthirties man wearing the black sport coat in front seemed to be the most hostile of the bunch, leaning heavily onto the front counter with both hands and glaring at the young woman.

"What's going on here?" Keith asked, stepping into the fray.

The front man turned to Keith. "You in charge?"

"Yes, Keith Bagley, the director. How can—"

"FBI," the man barked. "We need to speak with one of your new residents *right now*."

"Well, sir, we have certain protocols here. You can't just—"

The man interrupted again. "Did you not hear me say FBI?"

"Yes, I did, but—"

"Parker Barnes. Where is he?"

David stiffened. "Parker?"

The man turned to look at David. "You work here?"

David shook his head. "No, but—"

"Then this doesn't concern you."

"I beg to differ. I'm Parker's lawyer."

The man's face slowly bunched up. "Are you kidding me? You're the kid's lawyer?"

"Yes. David Adams."

If the FBI agent was trying to hide the fact that an attorney was the last thing he wanted to deal with right now, he failed miserably. The man let out a disgruntled sigh and rolled his tongue around in his mouth like he was trying to keep himself from vomiting.

"What's going on?" David asked.

"I'm Special Agent Harry Zegers," he finally said, and then introduced the other men with him in rapid fire as Agents Farley, Jeter, and Hernandez. They were all guys around David's age. "So, you're the one who got the kid out of the detention center before we could get over there this morning and speak to him. How the hell does a runaway like Parker even have an attorney, anyway?"

"That's really none of your business."

"*Everything* is our business."

"You might want to check your little FBI book again." David wasn't going to be intimidated by this guy or his little posse. Clearly, Zegers's strategy was to bull-rush his way into the building and make sure he got whatever he wanted, regardless of the facility's strict privacy and security policies. "Why do you want to talk with my client?"

"Because the kid is connected to the killing of a federal witness five days ago over in Pease Park."

That statement stunned David. "What? How?"

"That's why we need to chat with him. Find out what he knows."

"This is ludicrous. He's just a kid."

"So what? Kids are killers these days. Don't you watch the news?"

David's head was spinning. He now recalled seeing something a couple of days ago about the death of a federal witness. The man had been shot multiple times in the park and found the next morning. But Parker? A killer? No way.

"You can't possibly think Parker shot that man."

Zegers shrugged. "Until I talk with him, I'm ruling nothing out."

"How are you even putting him at the scene?"

Zegers turned, snapped his fingers at one of his cronies, who quickly pulled something up on an iPad and handed it to him. Zegers pushed "Play" and gave it to David. "This video was taken from a gas station security camera about a hundred yards away from the crime scene at the exact same time we're estimating for the death. We've been searching for your client ever since. One of the deputies at the detention center matched him with a photo we'd sent out a few days ago."

It was a grainy video that looked to be from a security camera above one of the gas pumps. The view caught the majority of the pumps below, the corner of the building, and the side parking lot. There were a couple of people casually standing at the pumps, staring at their phones, waiting for their cars to fill up.

David squinted. "I don't see anything relevant."

"Wait for it," Zegers instructed.

A second later, someone suddenly appeared from the wooded area on the other side of the parking lot. Looked like a boy in a T-shirt and blue jeans, carrying a backpack. The boy immediately took a tumble, rolled several times out onto the concrete. For a second, he sat there, staring into the woods behind him. Then he got back on his feet, took off running again—but zigzagging oddly as he did—until he got closer to the camera. He sprinted underneath the camera by the gas pumps and disappeared from view.

David wasn't convinced. "That could be any boy. You can't really see his face. Why do you think it's Parker?"

Zegers snatched the iPad away from him, pulled up a photo, then showed David an enhanced close-up still shot of the boy's face. "You're telling me that's not Parker Barnes, buddy?"

David hid his surprise. He had to admit the boy looked *a lot* like Parker. Still, it was a fuzzy shot that caught only part of the boy's face. Plus, these agents were acting like they wanted to throw Parker in a dark room right now, blind him with a bright light, and interrogate the hell out of him. David would never let that happen.

"I don't know," David countered. "Boys his age tend to all look the same. It's not definitive, if you ask me."

"Do you think a grand jury would find it definitive?"

David tilted his head. "You can't be serious."

"Look, David, let's not make this difficult. How about we just go ask him together? Let's find out where Parker was the night in question. If you're right and we're wrong, we can put this all behind us."

David gave the agents another quick glance. They looked like a pack of hyenas wanting to go after a vulnerable animal.

"I'll go talk to Parker. You guys wait here."

David sat alone with Parker in a small classroom.

The kid was all smiles. "You should see this computer software, Mr. Adams. I can take a picture of myself with the computer's camera and then put it on the face of a superhero I created. Then I get to be the main character in this video game. It's *so cool*."

"That's great," David said. "I'm glad you're already having fun."

"Yeah. Maybe this place ain't so bad."

David pressed his lips together, his forehead tightening. "Hey, I need to talk to you about something."

The smile on the boy's face instantly vanished. "What's wrong? Am I in trouble? Did I do something?"

David was disheartened at how quickly Parker had shifted from a state of joy to one of fear and trepidation. Reminded him of a rescued puppy that would cower in the corner every time someone in the room made a sudden move. This was probably a condition Parker had developed after years of feeling betrayed by the system. David hated that for the boy. It made him angry to even have to bring this up right now. But Zegers wasn't going away.

"No, it's nothing like that," David said, forcing a smile, trying to help Parker relax. "I just need to ask you some questions, that's all."

"Okay."

"Parker, where have you been staying at night this past week?"

The kid shrugged. "Wherever I can find a warm spot where someone doesn't mess with me. Why?"

"Do you remember where you were five nights ago?"

Parker shifted a bit. "Uh, not really. I think I probably stayed over by the Methodist church on the UT campus. That's where a lot of the guys I've been hanging around stay at night. They serve breakfast at the church a couple of days a week."

"You ever stay in Pease Park?"

Parker noticeably swallowed. "No."

"That's not too far away from campus. You sure?"

"I don't know. Maybe."

"There was a man who was shot over in Pease Park the other night. Do you know anything about that?"

David watched the boy closely.

Parker quickly shook his head. "Why're you asking me?"

"Well, some men are here from the FBI who want to talk with you about it. They seem to think you might have been around the park that night when this guy was shot."

Parker's eyes went wide. "The FBI?"

"Yes. But you don't need to be concerned."

"I don't want to talk to them, Mr. Adams."

"Why? They're the good guys."

"They won't believe me, no matter what I say."

"That's not true."

"Yes it is, Mr. Adams. I watched that movie *The Fugitive* with my dad. The guy on the run was innocent, but the FBI didn't believe him. So he had to keep running."

"Well, that was the US Marshals, not the FBI. And it was just a movie."

"Still . . . why do they want to talk to me? I don't know anything."

"They have a video of a boy running close to the park who looks a little bit like you."

Parker's eyes again widened. "It ain't me, I swear."

David tried to be reassuring. "You can talk to me, Parker. As your lawyer, I don't have to share *anything* you say with them. You're safe with me, okay?"

"It wasn't me, Mr. Adams. I'm not lying!"

The boy's eyes began watering, and his bottom lip started to quiver. David put his hand on Parker's shoulder and squeezed. Although he wasn't sure what the truth was, David wasn't interested in bringing on any more trauma today. Screw the FBI. He would take the heat for the boy. And deal with the fallout tomorrow.

"Hey, I believe you, okay? I'll take care of it. Don't worry."

David returned to the main lobby and found Zegers and his squad of look-alikes standing in a tight circle. Keith was still waiting next to the receptionist, clearly not wanting to leave her alone with the FBI. They all turned to David with anticipation. David swallowed, cleared his throat. The last thing he needed right now was for his voice to crack like a pubescent teenager's.

"Sorry, Harry. There will be no chats with my client today."

Zegers threw up his arms. "You've got to be kidding me!"

"I'm afraid not. But thanks for stopping by."

Zegers stepped close to David. So close, David thought he could smell maple syrup on the man's breath.

"You don't want to go toe-to-toe with me, David."

"This isn't about you and me."

"What's he hiding? If he's unwilling to talk with us, the boy clearly knows something about what happened that night. Why won't he talk?"

"This was actually my decision."

The agent shook his head. "You're only delaying the inevitable here. I'll get a subpoena. I'll force the boy to talk to us."

"Good luck with that."

Zegers turned, snapped his fingers, and the whole group of them stormed out the front door to the parking lot. David exhaled for the first time.

Keith walked over to him. "Well, that kind of thing doesn't happen around here every day."

"Sorry for the intrusion, Keith."

"No, it's okay. That guy was a jerk. How's Parker?"

"I'm not sure. He seems rattled."

"I'll keep my eye on him all day."

"Thanks." David watched as a black Tahoe filled with FBI agents tore out of the parking lot and then turned back to Keith. "Hey, promise me that no one from that crew talks with Parker without me knowing about it first."

"Don't worry. We're as protective as you are of our kids."

SEVEN

David returned to the office and found his feisty new pro bono investigator comfortably reclining in his office chair, a file in her hands and her black high heels resting on top of his messy desk.

"Please, make yourself at home," David quipped, slipping out of his suit jacket and hanging it on a coatrack by the door.

"Well, it's not like you have another office available to me in this dust bowl. A girl has to sit somewhere and work."

David grinned. "Did you have your own office over at Rossali, Meekins, and Tobian?"

"Of course. With a high-end glass desk, a plush leather office chair, three computer monitors, *and* a flat-screen TV on the wall. The works."

David whistled. "Nice."

"I'm sure you had something even better at Hunter and Kellerman. That firm spends way more than Rossali on over-the-top luxury."

"You investigating me now?"

"Don't flatter yourself. A quick Google search. Why'd you leave?"

He shrugged. "Long story. Let's just say my former boss did way more than grab my ass. You got anything for me?"

David had called Jess immediately upon leaving the Hand-Up Home to fill her in on his tricky situation with Parker and the FBI. He asked her to dig up whatever she could about crime scene details and the FBI's investigation into the death of the federal witness. Jess pulled her heels off the desk, stood, and began slowly pacing the office while ticking off details from memory.

"The dead guy is Max Legley, a fifty-two-year-old businessman. Legley was shot twice in the chest and once in the head, all at close range, about fifty feet away from a small parking lot at the south end of Pease District Park. An early-morning dog walker discovered the body and called 911. Legley was dressed in running shoes, black jogging pants, and a maroon windbreaker. Legley's vehicle, a late-model Cadillac Escalade, was still parked in the lot. Police found his cell phone sitting in the cupholder. There were twelve missed calls—all from Legley's wife. That's about all I could gather about the crime scene itself."

"What do you know about the federal case?"

"Legley and his business partner, Rick Kingston, both had been charged with federal tax fraud. They owned several restaurants around town. Feds got Legley to turn on Kingston. He was set to testify in court two days ago. But of course, that didn't happen. The federal prosecutor got the trial temporarily delayed. Legley's wife says her husband was paranoid that his former business partner might do something drastic to keep him from testifying. He was worried about their safety. Kingston's lawyer denies his client had anything to do with the death."

David stepped in front of his second-story office window and stared out over Congress Avenue. The downtown lunch crowd was out, and the sidewalks were growing busy. Jess moved in right next to him, also watching the crowd. With the high heels, she was about the same height as David. Her straight black hair came down just past her shoulders. He took in a whiff of her fragrance, which caught him off guard. It was the same perfume worn by his ex-girlfriend Jen Cantwell, who had moved back home to Virginia last year. Although it had been nearly a year, he still hadn't gotten over her yet.

"You ever have any dealings with the FBI?" he asked Jess.

"Sure. All the time back in DC. Why are they after this kid?"

"They think he was at the crime scene around the same time the guy was shot. They showed me footage from a security camera at a gas station near Pease Park. A boy who looks like Parker runs out of the woods from a trail that connects right back to that very spot in the park."

"Is it Parker?"

"He denies it, but I suspect he may be lying."

"Why would he lie about it?"

"I don't know. He doesn't trust easily. Can't blame him. The FBI agent I spoke with told me he considers Parker a suspect until proven otherwise."

"A twelve-year-old hit man?"

"I'm sure it was a bully tactic to scare me into cooperating."

"Did it work?"

"Almost," he admitted. "The guy was super aggressive."

"The feds can be ruthless when it comes to these situations. I once watched them toss a mother in jail back in Maryland when they believed she was hiding her daughter. The daughter wasn't even a suspect. Just a potential witness. A lot of it depends on the agent in charge."

"Well, this guy Zegers seems ready to hang Parker by a rope Old West–style *before* asking him any questions."

"Harry Zegers?"

He turned with a raised eyebrow. "You know him?"

She laughed, rolled her eyes. "Sort of. I went out on a blind date with him a few months ago. A friend of a friend set us up. She thought we might get along because we have similar investigative backgrounds. She couldn't have been more wrong. What an egomaniac. He talked about himself the entire time. He hardly asked me any questions. The guy actually thought it would be cute to order my meal for me before I cut him off with the waiter. I can order my own damn food, thank you very much."

"Sounds like him. A real charmer."

"You better not let on that I'm working with you."

"Why's that?"

A mischievous grin crossed her lips. "I faked illness during the date and got the hell out of there. I couldn't take one more second listening to that guy blab on about himself. He called me for a week, but I never answered. The guy just couldn't take a hint, I guess. I finally had to block him."

David smiled. "Real classy. But can't say I blame you."

"Yeah, well, I'm not sure I'm ready to date yet, anyway."

"Bad breakup or something?"

"Or something," she said, but didn't expound. "So, what are you going to do about the boy?"

"Figure out how to best protect him if Zegers somehow comes back with a grand jury subpoena. I can't let him go after Parker. That kid has been through hell already without having to deal with a buffoon like Zegers."

"Yeah, I read his file. Parker has definitely been through the wringer."

"Where did you get his file?"

"Doc gave me a copy. I like him. He's a cool cat."

"Then I guess you don't despise all homeless people, Jess."

"Doc? Seriously?"

David nodded. "He hit a rough stretch ten years ago, lost everything, and it's taken him a long time to finally get back on his feet. Believe it or not, the streets are filled with a lot of bad-luck guys just like him."

"Yeah, well, the streets are also filled with violent wackos."

"Some," he admitted.

"So, what can I do to help you with Parker?" Jess asked. "I kind of like the thought of kicking Harry Zegers's ass on this thing."

"Do you think you can get me a copy of the video he showed me? I want to examine it more closely."

"Yep. That's why you're paying me the big bucks."

EIGHT

Special Agent Harry Zegers was nearing his ten-year anniversary with the FBI but had felt stuck in the mud for the last three years—ever since he'd been placed on probation for using excessive force with a potential suspect. After breaking a lowlife weasel's nose in an outburst of anger, Zegers had gotten benched and seen countless job promotions come and go without hearing his name called. At thirty-seven, Zegers had fully expected to have moved up the FBI ranks by now. He thought he'd already be living in DC, where he'd be supervising terrorist investigations, or traveling to foreign lands on matters of national security.

While admittedly not as book smart or as educated as some of his colleagues—Zegers didn't have an Ivy League degree like a few of them—he was more hardworking and driven than most. So he was beyond frustrated that he'd stalled out at the FBI's Austin office, where he'd been heading up a long list of mindless investigations the past few years that were never going to get him noticed by anyone that mattered.

All had seemed bleak for him—until five days ago.

That's when the key witness for a federal fraud case had turned up dead. The case itself wasn't exactly high profile or demanding of national media attention. But Mark Anderson, the assistant US attorney handling it, was even more ambitious than Zegers. Anderson had managed to conjure up some local media coverage over the past few months and seemed to be enjoying his time smiling for the cameras. The guy clearly had big career aspirations. However, with his key witness gone, Anderson was now desperate to keep his case from completely unraveling. He was damn near begging Zegers to dig up some answers for him quickly to get his trial back on track. He had even promised to get the FBI agent noticed in the right circles. Because of that, Zegers had been working nonstop on the case. He'd barely slept in four days and was driving his guys hard. This was his chance finally to put the probation behind him and move forward in his career.

Zegers sat in a corner booth at Kerbey Lane Cafe, waiting for Anderson to join him for a late lunch. A half-eaten cheeseburger sat on the table. Wearing a black sport coat and slacks, Zegers had his eyes on a set of reports in his hands. He ran a hand through his thick black hair while holding a report farther away from his eyes. He needed to start wearing reading glasses but thought they made him look weak. He was only in his late thirties, after all. Zegers couldn't afford to look weak right now. That's why he still hit the gym and pumped weights almost every day—a workout schedule that had become easier to manage six months ago after his ex-wife, Lisa, gained full custody of their fourteen-year-old son, Josh. The judge had agreed with her that Zegers's continued fits of anger and irrational behavior posed an ongoing threat to his job status, which, of course, would impact his ability to properly care for his son.

Zegers was still pissed. And even more determined to get a promotion now to prove both the judge and Lisa dead wrong. They'd married as kids while at Auburn. Lisa was an aspiring fashion designer. Zegers thought he was destined to make it to the major leagues as a second baseman. He had both the athletic ability and the good looks to attract potential endorsement deals. He'd gotten as far as Double-A ball before leading the league in strikeouts in back-to-back years because he couldn't hit the damn slider. Teams basically gave up on him after that. The disappointment led to anger, which led to drinking. They'd barely survived that first round of marriage turmoil. Lisa hung in there because of their son, who was four at the time. Zegers finally pulled it together and went the law enforcement route by joining the FBI. Life was good for a little while, as he easily got promoted. But when he lost steam three years ago, the drinking started again, and so did all the fighting. He couldn't really blame Lisa for wanting out. He could be a stubborn ass. But he missed her. And he missed the hell out of Josh, who didn't seem to be all that interested in a relationship with his father at the moment.

Mark Anderson finally arrived. The federal prosecutor was tall and skinny with brown hair that was already thinning, even though he was probably five years younger than Zegers. Word on the street was that the attorney was wicked smart. Zegers knew Anderson had gotten his undergrad at Duke and his law degree from Harvard. His father was some kind of big-deal lobbyist in DC. Anderson also was the current golden child of Jim Dozier, the US attorney for the Western District of Texas. His future was bright, which was why Zegers was eager to hitch a ride with him.

Taking off his gray suit jacket, Anderson slid into the booth. "Please tell me you have something for me, Harry. What did the boy say?"

Zegers had given Anderson a heads-up earlier that they'd finally found the mystery boy in the security video and were on their way to speak with him. It had been the only positive lead they'd had on this case so far.

"Ran into problems," Zegers admitted.

"What kind of problems?"

"The kid has a damn lawyer."

"So what? Work with the lawyer."

"I tried. The lawyer is an ass."

Anderson sighed. "What did you do, Harry?"

"Nothing. He wouldn't let the boy talk to me. So I told him I'd get a grand jury subpoena and make him talk."

"Please tell me you didn't actually say that."

"Why? Can't you get the subpoena? The boy is the same as in the video. We know it's him. We know he was there when Legley was killed. Let's make him talk."

Anderson cursed, shook his head. "No grand jury is going to force a kid to testify based on a video showing him near the vicinity where Legley was shot. I would need something much more concrete connecting the kid to the actual crime scene. I can't believe you threatened the lawyer with that. You should've handled the whole thing with velvet gloves and not boxing gloves."

"Well, velvet gloves aren't my style."

"And look where that got you."

Zegers exhaled in frustration. He knew Anderson was right. He'd made a stupid tactical error. "I'll keep working on the attorney."

"You'd better. We're running out of time here. I'm going to have to drop this whole damn case if you can't turn up any answers soon. That won't be good for either one of our careers."

"We're not sitting around on our asses, okay? We're out there hustling."

"Yeah, I hear ya. But Dozier is all over me right now. He blames me for not making sure Legley was better protected."

"He's not wrong, you know."

"I guess. But I just never believed one of these guys was capable of cold-blooded murder. Hell, they're just two rich suburban white guys who didn't pay their damn taxes. Not mobsters."

"We still have no proof yet that Kingston is behind it."

"Don't remind me. But we all know he did it. There has to be something we're missing. Have you interrogated him again?"

"Three different times. His story has remained consistent."

"He's going to crack eventually."

"Maybe. But I can't waterboard him to make it happen, okay?"

"That's too bad. It would make this a whole lot easier."

Zegers shook his head, took a bite of his cheeseburger. Anderson was correct that Kingston was the clear suspect in the death of his former business partner. The man was facing a minimum of five years in prison. After her husband's death four days ago, Christina Legley had told the FBI that her husband was growing concerned that Kingston might try to do something drastic. She said her husband told her Kingston had once before talked about hiring someone to "take out" a problem when one of their restaurant managers had threatened to sue them over harassment. At the time, Legley had thought he was joking, but his former business partner had insisted he wasn't and that he knew a guy who would do the job for a price.

The night that Legley died, Kingston was at a banquet surrounded by dozens of witnesses. According to Christina Legley, her husband had gotten a phone call around nine thirty the night of his death. He told her he had to run out and take care of something. He got into his Cadillac Escalade and drove away. He never came home. Zegers had discovered the call had originated from a burner phone purchased with cash earlier that day at a store with no security cameras. The trail had gone cold from there.

His cell phone buzzed in his pants pocket. Zegers checked the display. It was Agent Farley, his top lieutenant.

"What's up?" Zegers answered.

"Where are you?"

"Lunch. Why?"

"We found the boy's backpack."

Zegers raced back to the office, where Farley was waiting for him inside a small conference room. At first appearance, Farley didn't seem like much. He was only five-seven with a slender build, a crew cut of blond hair, pale skin, and a boyish face. Farley looked like he might have just graduated from high school. But his looks were deceiving. A former All-American wrestler at Iowa, Farley was as tough as they came. Zegers had seen him take down two perps all by himself. He was also very loyal to Zegers. There had been several incidents where Zegers had crossed the line out in the field, and Farley had not reported anything to his superiors.

A dirty black backpack sat on top of the table with its contents spread out. Earlier that day, Zegers had ordered a crew to search the entire area around the location where Parker Barnes had been arrested for stealing purses the night before in hopes of finding this very item. The boy didn't have the backpack when police caught him.

It was a long shot that had actually paid off.

"Where was it?" he asked Farley.

"Hidden in the bushes behind Shady Grove."

Zegers nodded. Shady Grove was one of many restaurants that sat along Barton Springs Road.

"How do you know it's his?" he asked.

Wearing latex gloves, Farley picked up a small photo off the table and held it up for Zegers to view. A boy who was clearly a younger version of Parker Barnes was standing next to a man who was probably his father. Both of them were smiling big. It looked like they were at an amusement park together. For the first time, Zegers felt a little sad for the boy. Although Zegers had had a rocky relationship with his own father growing up, he couldn't have imagined losing him at such a young age. But he also couldn't let these feelings distract him from the mission at hand. Right now, the boy might be critical to solving this case. Which was critical to advancing his own broken career and earning back partial custody of his son.

Zegers quickly pulled on his own latex gloves and began picking through the backpack's items—which had all been inserted into clear, resealable bags. A stick of deodorant, hand sanitizer, toothbrush, and toothpaste. A worn paperback copy of *Harry Potter and the Sorcerer's Stone*. Black headphones but no devices to plug them into. Three packages of granola bars and two small packages of Skittles. A small bottle half filled with water. Several pens and a spiral-bound notebook mostly filled with drawings of comic-book-type characters. Three pairs of stained white socks. Two pairs of tighty-whities. Blue gym shorts. A red hooded sweatshirt. A black T-shirt with the Houston Rockets logo. A plain white T-shirt. A gray T-shirt. That was about it.

Zegers stared at the bags with the T-shirts. "What color was the shirt the kid was wearing in the video?"

"Gray, I think," Farley said.

Zegers picked up the bag with the gray T-shirt and pulled it out to examine it more closely. It was dirt stained all over, with a hole in the shoulder. On the very front was a red circular stain about the size of a small fist. Zegers held it up close to his eyes, and a small smile crossed his lips.

"Is that a bloodstain?" Farley asked.

"Could be. Get this to the lab ASAP. Let's see if we got a match for the victim."

NINE

Richie Maylor stood alone on the banks of the Colorado River, smoking a cigarette. At twenty-six, Richie had accomplished very little in life—unless anyone counted his growing list of misdemeanors, plus the second-degree felony assault that had left him sitting in a prison cell for eighteen months. He'd just recently lost his part-time job driving a forklift over at a junkyard. The constant drinking and his short temper had made it hard for any business owner to put up with him for too long. So he'd been doing odd jobs here and there to make just enough cash to keep up with rent on his dump of an RV trailer parked a mile up the road. Most of the jobs involved chasing down idiots who owed his boss money.

However, Richie's latest assignment was much bigger than that. His boss had offered to pay him a significant cash bonus—hell, enough to pay off his trailer and maybe even put new wheels on his truck. Everything had gone as planned until that damn kid had shown up out of nowhere. Had the boy seen the whole thing? Did the boy overhear anything Richie had said to the guy? Richie had stupidly run his mouth a bit, even mentioning his boss by name, before pulling the trigger. He couldn't be sure what the kid had heard. And he hadn't been fast enough to catch that stupid kid and find out. Now he was sitting in hot water because of it. His boss was not a happy man.

Richie cursed at that thought, which had kept him from sleeping well the past few nights. He finished his cigarette, flicked it away, and quickly lit up another. Richie turned when his boss walked down a dirt trail to meet him a few minutes later. In his fifties, his boss was trim, clean-shaven, with a head of thick, wavy brown hair. Wearing a tan suit and white dress shirt without a tie, his boss had the good looks of an aging movie star. He was always dressed in nice suits and driving expensive cars. Under any other circumstances, Richie would not be intimidated by the man. After all, Richie was stacked with lean muscles from a childhood mostly spent baling hay every day for his abusive stepdad. Richie had even survived attacks by prison gangs. But he knew his boss was someone to be feared. Richie had heard his boss was connected to a local criminal network that ran an underground gambling ring. There were rumors that his boss had even had someone killed a couple of years ago for betraying him.

Richie had never really believed that rumor—until a few days ago.

He swallowed the lump in his throat as his boss made his way over to him. For a second, the man didn't say anything. Instead, he pulled his own cigarette from a carton, lit it with a lighter, and started puffing while staring at the river. The silence made Richie shift awkwardly. His boss had ordered him to remain completely off the radar for the past five days. So that's exactly what Richie had done—until his boss had texted him today and told him to meet here. Richie knew that if his boss had hired him to do what he'd done five days ago, the man could just as easily have paid someone else to do the same to him. He'd already threatened it repeatedly because of what his boss had called a *massive screw-up*. Richie wondered if one of his boss's thugs was somewhere nearby. Because of this fear, Richie had his gun buried in the back of his jeans beneath his denim jacket.

"I might have just saved your ass," his boss finally said in between puffs. "And gotten you a second chance to make things right."

Richie exhaled, grateful to not have to try to shoot his way out of a sticky situation this morning. "How's that?"

His boss pulled his phone from a pocket inside his suit jacket, brought up a photo on the screen, and held it out in front of Richie. "This him? This the boy?"

Richie stared at the photo, which was a booking shot of a boy with unkempt brown hair wearing an orange juvie jumpsuit. It was definitely the same kid. He'd gotten a clear look at him in the bright glow of his truck headlights. Right before the boy had taken off like a rocket.

"That's him, boss. Where is he?"

"He got picked up for theft last night and taken over to the juvenile justice center on South Congress."

Richie knew the place well. He'd had his own brief stay there as a teenager after stealing a truck from his ex-girlfriend's brother. He would have rather remained there in juvie than to have been picked up by his angry stepdad, who then proceeded to beat him with his leather belt until Richie could barely walk. The old man had liver cancer now, and Richie couldn't wait for him to die. His stepdad always had treated his mom like a slave. Richie used to lie in bed at night as a kid and fantasize about grabbing a hammer, sneaking into his stepdad's bedroom, and bludgeoning him. But he never had the courage to do anything. Plus, he couldn't handle the thought of breaking his mom's heart. Somehow, she still loved that abuser.

His boss continued. "Judge released him to a midtown youth center today."

"What do you want me to do?" Richie asked.

"What the hell do you think?"

"I'll take care of it, boss."

"Good. Because if that boy somehow blows this up for all of us, you might as well take that gun you have hidden in the back of your pants, put it to your own head, and pull the damn trigger."

TEN

Parker spent the afternoon following Keith around the Hand-Up Home. The director seemed to be going over the top to make sure he felt welcome and comfortable. Parker didn't mind it. Whenever he'd been dumped into other foster facilities, they'd usually just thrown him into the mix and somehow expected him to easily adapt. That rarely happened. Not because Parker was incapable. But there was always a pecking order among the kids at these places. And the boys who ran the show usually tried to make sure right away that any new kids fell in line. He knew that day would soon arrive here. But it was nice for Parker to not have to immediately start watching his back.

Around midafternoon, all the boys were released into the courtyard for an hour of playtime. A big group of them headed over to the basketball court. Several of the younger kids hit the playground. Parker mostly hung by himself. He wasn't ready to interact with the others just yet. He wanted to get the lay of the land first. See if he could begin to identify the alpha kids—those who might pose a threat to him. Plus, he couldn't stop thinking about what Mr. Adams had said earlier regarding the FBI wanting to talk to him. That scared the crap out of him. Where did they get a video? Did they for sure know he was there when it happened?

He wondered if Mr. Adams would truly be able to take care of it. Did he actually believe Parker? Could he keep the FBI away? Parker wanted to call him and ask him more about it—just to try to calm his own nerves—but he figured that would only draw more suspicion onto himself. Parker didn't want to screw this up. He hated lying to Mr. Adams because he really liked him. The man reminded him a lot of his dad. They were around the same height and weight and had similar brown hair. Both of them also had an easygoing manner about them. Even the way Mr. Adams had put his hand on Parker's shoulder earlier to comfort him was similar to what his dad used to do when Parker was all worked up about something.

And, Mr. Adams was going to take him to the football game next Saturday. No way did he want to mess that up. Parker hoped if he just played it cool, everything would be okay.

After watching some of the other guys play basketball for a little while, Parker made his way over to the corner of the courtyard next to the tall wrought-iron fence. He watched cars going up and down the street and then spotted a young guy out by the stoplight wearing saggy jeans and a white tank top, holding a cardboard sign asking for money. Parker thought he recognized the guy from the group of runaway teenagers he'd been hanging around with recently. Jester? Jericho? He couldn't remember his name right now.

Parker had to admit it was nice to have walked straight into Hand-Up's big cafeteria earlier and received a tray filled with good food. Instead of begging, stealing, or walking miles across the city for a crappy free meal. The bed in his new room felt soft, and the covers were clean. Parker was on the top bunk. But the kid in the bottom bunk offered to switch if Parker was more comfortable below. The boy's name was Grayson. He was a year younger than Parker and seemed okay. Parker said he was fine on top. He actually looked forward to going to sleep tonight for the first time in a really long time.

Parker's thoughts were suddenly interrupted by a husky voice coming from the shadows on the other side of the protective courtyard fence.

"Hey there, Parker."

Parker squinted but didn't spot anyone at first.

"Over here."

Parker moved closer to the fence, then let out an audible gasp. His throat closed up, and his legs locked in place. He couldn't believe it. Standing ten feet away from him, beneath the shade of a tree, was the same guy who had chased him through the woods with a gun the other night. He immediately recognized the goatee and the jean jacket. He would never forget the guy's face. The man was puffing on a cigarette and letting the smoke slowly leak out a corner of his mouth. A sinister smile spread across the guy's face as he stepped even closer to the fence. They were now only five feet apart—just the fence between them—and Parker felt his bladder wanting to give out.

"Remember me, kid?"

Parker knew he should immediately turn and run like hell. Go find Keith and tell him everything. But he couldn't get his feet to move. He felt paralyzed. Was this real? Was the guy actually standing there and talking to him? How could this be happening? It didn't make any sense. How could the guy have found him? The goateed man pulled his jacket slightly open, revealing a gun shoved into the front of his blue jeans.

He blew cigarette smoke toward Parker. "You better keep your damn mouth shut, kid, if you know what's good for you. I can get to you in here. I can get to you anywhere. You understand me?"

A couple of younger boys kicked a soccer ball into the corner of the courtyard near him. This seemed to make the man uneasy. He quickly closed his jacket, took several steps away from the fence. Parker finally got his legs moving. He began slowly stumbling backward, but his eyes never left the guy. Then the man made a finger gun with his right hand, aimed it at him, and pulled the trigger. Parker turned and ran as fast as he could through the courtyard toward the building while trying hard to not piss his own pants.

ELEVEN

David rolled over in his bed, grabbed his phone off the nightstand, and squinted at it with blurry eyes. Keith? From Hand-Up Home? Calling him at three in the morning? What the hell? David suddenly thought of Parker, felt a chill move through him, and quickly answered.

"Hey, man, everything okay?"

"You better get over here, David," Keith said.

"What happened?"

Keith sighed. "Parker ran away."

David sat straight up in bed. "You're kidding?"

"I'm afraid not. I've got the police here now."

"I'll be right there."

After throwing on a pair of blue jeans, a T-shirt, and his brown leather jacket, David jumped into his truck and sped through near-empty city streets straight to the youth facility. A steady rain was now coming down. David had been hearing the thunder throughout the night. Two police cars were parked in front of the building. He hopped out of his truck, sloshed through the rain, and found Keith standing inside the main lobby speaking with one of the officers. It looked like a couple of staff members were also there.

Keith excused himself and made his way over to David.

"What the hell happened?" David asked.

"Better I show you rather than try to explain."

Keith led David into a small room close by that had eight security TV monitors hanging on a wall above a desk. Sitting in a swivel chair, Keith began typing on a keyboard and said the monitors were for eight different cameras located around the facility—monitoring the cafeteria, the courtyard, the hallways, and the activity rooms.

"Watch the fourth camera," Keith said. "This was about forty minutes ago."

David leaned in from behind the director and spotted Parker stepping into the hallway fully clothed. The boy looked in both directions. The hallway was completely empty. Parker crept down the hallway to his right and carefully walked past the other rooms. When he reached the end of the hallway, a second camera picked him up from the opposite direction. David studied the boy's face. He looked scared but determined. Parker tried to open the door to what Keith explained was the cafeteria. Then he tried another door to the courtyard. Turning around, Parker made his way back down the hallway to the opposite end. David watched as Parker tried to open another door that was also locked. David remembered that all the doors in the facility were secured and needed electronic card keys. The boy stared intently through the window in the door. Then Parker knocked on the hallway door a couple of times and tucked back away out of sight. What was he doing? After slowly peeking around, Parker knocked again. Another glance through the window. Then the boy slipped inside the first bedroom and outside camera shot.

"We don't have cameras in the bedrooms, of course," Keith mentioned. Then he pointed at another camera. "This is Tucker. He works on our night staff."

David watched as a pudgy guy wearing a black polo shirt and blue jeans made his way toward the door on the opposite side of the hallway from where Parker had been knocking. He used his card key, opened the door, and stepped into the same hallway. For a second, he paused, looked around. David swallowed, hoping he wasn't about to see Parker do something really foolish. Tucker took a peek inside the same room where Parker had disappeared. David held his breath. But thankfully, nothing happened. Parker must've somehow hid out of sight. Then Tucker made his way to the next bedroom, looked inside, and ambled over to the third bedroom. That's when Parker made his reappearance. He stepped back into the hallway, slipped in behind Tucker undetected, and suddenly snagged something from the guy's side.

"That's Tucker's card key," Keith clarified. "It was clipped to his belt."

Tucker turned around, said something, but Parker was already running away. The kid made his way back to the hallway door, opened it with the card key, and quickly pushed it shut behind him just before Tucker could get there. It looked like Parker might've said something to Tucker through the door window. Then David watched Parker run down other hallways, through several more security doors, flying past another unwitting female staff member, before he finally escaped out the front doors. Parker's last few seconds on camera showed him tucking his head against the pounding of raindrops before he disappeared.

And that was that. Parker was gone.

Keith turned to him. "Tucker called me right away."

David cursed, shook his head. "I don't get it, Keith. Did something happen to provoke him?"

"I don't think so. I was with him most of the day yesterday. He seemed fine, although he kind of closed up on me toward the end of the day. I figured he was just worn out by everything that had happened."

"Did Parker steal something? Why're the cops here?"

"Just standard protocol. We have to call them when something like this happens. I'm not aware that he stole anything. Tucker actually told me Parker said he was sorry to him through the door window after locking him inside the hallway."

David sighed. "This doesn't make any sense. Parker swore to my face that he wouldn't cause any trouble. I don't understand why he'd do this."

"Kids are unpredictable, David. Especially kids like Parker."

"Maybe. But I can usually read people well."

Keith shrugged. "I don't know what to tell you. I'm sorry this happened."

"No, I'm the one who should be apologizing. You did me a favor. And all I've brought you since yesterday morning is a big headache. First, the FBI. Now this. I'm just glad no one got hurt."

David climbed back into his truck after speaking with the two officers and informing them he knew nothing about Parker's current whereabouts. He asked if they would call him if the boy turned up somewhere. Everyone agreed they just wanted him safe and off the streets. He sat there for a moment, again trying to make sense of what had happened. Why would Parker run? The kid seemed genuinely happy about being there. David knew he wasn't faking it. The kid wore his emotions on his sleeve. Had their conversation about the FBI spooked him so badly that he made a run for it? David considered it. Could Parker have actually had something to do with the man's death in the park? A sinking feeling hit his gut. Had he completely misread the kid?

David checked the time on his cell phone. Four in the morning. He wondered how long it would take before Harry Zegers came bursting through his door, giving him hell. With his eyes on his phone, David spotted a voice mail notification. He tapped the icon and found a twenty-two-second message from a random number left just over an hour ago—right before Keith had woken him up. He hadn't noticed it before now since he'd been in such a rush to get over to the facility.

He pressed "Play" and listened. It was Parker's shaky voice.

"Mr. Adams, this is Parker . . . I'm, uh, so sorry . . . I, uh . . . I had to leave the Hand-Up Home . . . I really wanted to stay there, like I promised you . . . but I couldn't. Someone . . . I, uh, I can't say, or he'll hurt me bad, but I just had to get out of there . . . I'm sorry . . . I really wanted to go to the game with you next Saturday . . . sucks that I can't now . . ."

The message ended. David listened to it again. Then a third time. His heart was pounding. Parker didn't run away tonight just because he was a rebellious kid. Something had happened. *He'll hurt me bad.* What was Parker talking about? Who would hurt him bad? David called the same number from the voice mail message, listened to it ring four times. Then it went to an automated greeting. Whose phone had Parker used? David left a brief message, identifying himself as an attorney, and asked whoever owned the phone to call him back ASAP.

Then he called Jess Raven.

TWELVE

David parked in front of a midtown brown-brick duplex off Forty-Fifth Street with a small front yard and a carport on the side that currently held a black Ford Explorer. Jess greeted David at the door with groggy eyes, wearing red flannel pajama shorts and a gray GO NAVY, BEAT ARMY T-shirt. She had her black hair pulled up into a messy bun and was sporting stylish, black-rimmed glasses. David thought she looked attractive even in her early-morning getup. Although she was seriously frowning at him right now.

"Listen, buddy, I don't know what you think 'pro bono' buys you these days, but I promise you a four a.m. wake-up call is not part of the package."

"I'm sorry," he offered. "But this is urgent."

"Fine. Come in. But don't expect me to be nice."

She led him inside the duplex. A tiny living room with a sofa, a chair, and a small TV sat to the right. All neat and well decorated. There was a cool piece of abstract art hanging on the front wall with lots of blues and grays that looked kind of like a huge tidal wave exploding in the ocean. David noticed the initials *JMR* painted in the bottom-left corner.

Jessica Michelle Raven was her full legal name.

"Did you really paint that?" he asked her.

"Depends. You like it?"

"I love it."

"Then, yeah, I painted it."

"Wow. Didn't figure you as the artist type."

"My mom loves to paint. She's a terrific artist. So I dabbled with it some growing up. I picked it up again a couple of years ago as an outlet while going through a rough stretch."

"You should paint something for the office," he suggested.

"That place could definitely use it. But coffee first."

They went into the kitchen. A golden retriever came out of a back hallway and greeted David with tongue wagging.

"That's Bailey," Jess said. "She's more of a morning person."

"I can tell," David said, giving Bailey some vigorous petting.

"You want coffee?" Jess offered.

"Sure, if you're making it for yourself."

"Well, I won't be going back to bed after this. Once I get up, I'm up for good. Might as well get my day started."

David noticed a three-inch scar on her right thigh just above the knee.

"Gunshot," she said, following his eyes.

"For real? You've been shot?"

She nodded. "Suspect shot right through his front door my rookie year and caught me good. So I got to join an exclusive club early in my career."

"There's a club for getting shot?"

"Informal. I don't have, like, an official T-shirt or anything." She placed a pod in the Keurig. "What's so urgent?"

"Parker ran away from the children's home an hour ago."

She turned from the Keurig. "I thought you said that facility was on full lockdown."

"It is locked down. But he stole a staff member's card key right off him, locked the guy in the hallway, and then made a go for it through several more secured areas and out the front door. I watched the whole thing unfold on security cameras with Keith, the director, a few minutes ago."

"Well, that sucks. Why do you think he ran?"

"I don't know. But he left me this voice mail right after breaking out of there this morning. That's why I'm here."

David pulled out his phone and played her the message.

"That's interesting," Jess said. "How did he call you?"

"I'm not sure yet. I called the number back but didn't get an answer."

"I'll track down the number first thing." She brought him a cup of coffee along with creamer from the fridge. "What do you think he's talking about? Who's going to hurt him bad?"

David took a sip. "No clue. But something clearly happened after I left him there today. I can tell by the sound in his voice."

"You sure? You don't really know this kid that well."

"I'm sure, Jess. He may have been a bit worked up by our whole FBI conversation today. But listen to him now? He's moved beyond being upset. The boy leaving this message is straight up frightened."

"Maybe another kid there did something to him."

"Keith says he was with Parker for most of the day. He never witnessed anything and got no reports of such a thing. They watch these kids closely."

Jess made herself a cup of coffee, and then they both sat around the small kitchen table. The golden rested her head in David's lap, so he gave the dog more petting.

"Why do you think the kid called you?" Jess asked. "Seems like an odd thing to do right after breaking out of that place."

"I agree. Again, I have no idea. I don't know whether his running is tied to the death of this federal witness, but I don't like the idea of

Parker being out there on the streets while the FBI still wants to talk with him."

"Harry Zegers is going to give you absolute hell."

"Yeah, I'm surprised he's not banging on your front door right now."

"He better not be. I don't want that egomaniac at my house."

They shared a quick grin. She went back to the kitchen and began poking around in the fridge. On a buffet cabinet against the wall of the kitchen, David noticed several framed photographs of Jess with the same guy. One with them dressed in ski gear on a mountain. At the beach holding hands. Both kneeling next to a younger version of Bailey. In another photo, the guy was dressed in a full-on police uniform. A patch on his arm showed he worked for the DC Metropolitan Police Department. David wondered who he was since Jess had mentioned she didn't want to date *anyone* right now.

"My husband," she said, noticing his stares.

He turned to her. "You're married?"

"Not anymore. He died."

"Damn, Jess. I'm sorry. What happened?"

"He was killed in the line of duty. Jeff and his partner were breaking up a heated exchange between two sidewalk crazies near the Capitol building. It got physical. One of them somehow got ahold of Jeff's partner's gun and discharged a bullet. My husband died instantly. We'd just celebrated our one-year anniversary."

David put two and two together. Two sidewalk crazies? She must've meant two erratic homeless guys. Which would account for her current disdain for that community.

"I don't know what to say, Jess. I can't even—"

She cut him off. "I'm fine, really. It was three years ago." She quickly changed the subject. "You think Keith would let me review all of the facility's security footage from yesterday?"

"Probably. I'll definitely ask him."

"I'll go over there ASAP and see if I can spot anything unusual."

THIRTEEN

As expected, Harry Zegers showed up at David's office right as the sun was rising on the city. David's cell phone had been buzzing incessantly for the past thirty minutes. All calls he'd ignored. If Zegers wanted to curse him out, David was going to make the man at least go to a lot of effort to do it.

David was at his desk reviewing a file for another client when the pounding on the main office door rattled the walls. David made his way through the entry room, unlocked the door, and pulled it slightly back. Zegers was standing there scowling at him, along with one of his other agents.

"Good morning, Harry," David said. "Farley, is it?"

Zegers got right to it. "You really screwed this up, didn't you, David? You just had to play your lawyer games with me, and now we've all got a big mess on our hands. You're lucky that kid didn't hurt anyone."

"A normal person usually offers a 'good morning' in return."

Zegers ignored his quip. "Parker Barnes is clearly neck-deep in this whole damn thing, and now he's gone. Poof! Disappeared! Because of you!"

"You act like I drove the getaway car."

"Did you?"

David sighed. "Do you want to come inside, Harry? Or just stand there yelling at me from the hallway?"

David stepped out of the way and allowed both agents into the entry room. Farley immediately began sniffing around and poking his head into the other three rooms of the office suite.

"Do you really think Parker is hiding out here?" David asked Zegers.

Zegers crossed his arms. "We'll leave no stone unturned."

"Well, unless you have a search warrant, keep your crony in check."

Zegers gave Farley a subtle nod, and the younger agent settled back into the entry room while also glaring at David.

"Look, I don't know why he took off," David explained. "But that doesn't mean he's 'neck-deep,' as you say. The kid may just be a runner, which was how he ended up out on the streets in the first place."

"So you haven't heard from him?"

David was unsure how to answer that. On one hand, he wanted to find Parker and make sure he was safe. So any information he handed over might help with that. On the other hand, he didn't trust Zegers and his crew to handle Parker with the appropriate care right now. He felt caught between a rock and a hard place.

"You know I can't divulge privileged client information."

Zegers cursed. "Where is he?"

"I have no idea. I wish I did. I don't want the kid on the streets."

"Neither do I but probably for different reasons. Just so you know, that kid is now a full-on suspect. I don't care if he's twelve years old. We will hunt him down and treat him as if he's armed and dangerous."

"You've got to be kidding me."

Zegers grabbed his phone from his pocket, pulled something up on the screen, and showed it to David. "This is a photo of the shirt Parker was wearing the night in question. You see that circular stain right there on the front? It's blood. And it's not the kid's blood. The blood is a match for the dead guy in the park. I'd say that's 'neck-deep,' pal."

David felt punched in the gut with this news. It confirmed that Parker really had been at the scene of the crime the other night. "Where did you get the shirt?"

"You think we're small-town cops here, David? We've been out there investigating. We found Parker's backpack near where he got picked up for theft. By the way, it matches the backpack worn by the kid in the security video—the kid you claimed was not your client."

"I never said it wasn't my client. I said it was ambiguous."

"Well, it sure as hell isn't ambiguous anymore. The kid was there that night. Whether he was actually involved with the death, we still don't know yet—thanks to you. But we will certainly now pursue him as if he may have pulled the trigger himself."

"You need to settle down, Harry. He is still just a scared kid."

"Not in my eyes. I may have viewed him that way yesterday, *if* you'd allowed me to talk with him. But not anymore."

David felt a surge of panic push through him. The thought of a swarm of FBI agents out there hunting Parker down in the streets like a criminal scared the hell out of him. Maybe Zegers was right. Maybe he should have pushed harder yesterday to get Parker to tell him the truth about the scene in the video. Now the boy was in even more danger. Parker might get badly injured out there trying to run—or even worse.

"I'll do my best to help," David genuinely offered.

"You bet your ass you will," Zegers sneered. "Because if I find out that you're somehow aiding a suspect, I'll throw your ass in jail for obstruction of justice. And I'll take great pleasure in doing it."

As if the tension in the office wasn't already thick enough, Jess showed up at that moment. She walked inside the office with her work-bag in one hand and a small white sack in the other.

Everyone turned to stare at her.

"Looks like I'm late to the party," she said. She held up the white sack. "But I brought doughnuts, if that helps."

"Jess?" Zegers said, clearly surprised to see her.

She gave him a curt grin. "Oh, hey, Harry. How're you?"

"What are you doing here?"

Instead of just telling him the truth, Jess walked over to where David stood, gave him a quick peck on the cheek, and then turned back to Zegers. "Bringing my boyfriend breakfast. What about you?"

David watched as Zegers's whole face flushed red. The agent didn't respond to Jess; instead, he turned his attention back to David.

"I mean it, David. If you find out where that kid is hiding, you'd better pick up the phone and call me ASAP—or else I'll have your ass."

"Duly noted."

Zegers frowned at Jess and then stormed out with Farley on his heels.

Shutting the door behind them, David turned to Jess. "Was that really necessary? That guy already wants to rip my head off."

She shrugged. "I could tell he had you in a corner. I didn't like it."

David shook his head, smiled. "You really have doughnuts in there?"

She handed him the bag. "Help yourself."

"Thanks. I'm starving."

He pulled out a glazed doughnut and took a big bite.

"So, what did the blowhard have to say for himself?" Jess asked.

"He's now treating Parker like a suspect. They apparently found blood on the shirt Parker was wearing that night that matches the victim."

"Uh-oh. That's not good."

"No, it's not. Did you find out anything?"

Jess had been with Keith for the past couple of hours, searching through all of the facility security camera footage from yesterday.

"First off, Parker called you from a cell phone that he'd borrowed from a nineteen-year-old clerk named Lewis at a twenty-four-hour convenience store only four blocks away from the facility. The guy said a kid came into the store, claimed he was lost, needed to call his parents to come pick him up, and asked if he could borrow a phone. So the guy let him use his cell phone. He said the kid made a quick call in the corner of the store, gave him the phone back, real polite and all, and then left the store."

David finished off the doughnut. "Someone provoked him to make a run for it. You could tell he felt bad about it. He kept repeating how sorry he was in the voice mail."

"Agreed. And I think I found that *someone*." She pulled an iPad out of her black leather bag. "I tried to follow Parker's actions from the moment you left him there at the facility. As Keith told you, he was with Parker for most of the day. But not for all of it. This is footage of the courtyard when all the kids were outside running around and playing yesterday afternoon."

They huddled over the iPad together. The camera view was from the corner of the building. In the immediate foreground was the playground with the swing sets, climbing bars, and slides. The basketball court could be seen at a distance in the far-right corner of the screen. A grassy area was in the far-left corner of the screen leading up to the security fence.

Jess pointed at the screen. "That's Parker standing over there in the corner by the fence. Watch what happens next."

David squinted at the screen. For a moment, Parker was just standing there all by himself and kind of staring out toward the street. Then something seemed to get his attention. He turned, tilted his head, and took a couple of small steps forward to within a few feet of the fence. Suddenly, he visibly stiffened and stayed perfectly still.

"There," Jess said. "Look at this guy on the other side."

David leaned in farther. A guy with a goatee wearing a jean jacket stepped forward and stood directly across the fence from Parker. He looked like he was saying something, but Parker wasn't responding to him. Then the guy pulled his jacket back for a moment.

"What's the guy doing?" David asked.

"I don't know. I can't tell."

A couple of other boys kicked a soccer ball into the corner next to Parker. The man quickly closed his jacket and moved away from the fence. At this point, Parker began to take slow steps backward, almost tripping himself up because he wouldn't stop staring at the guy. David could tell Parker was all tensed up about whatever had just happened.

Jess pointed at the screen again. "The guy makes some kind of hand gesture right here. And then points at Parker."

David watched as Parker then turned and ran really fast through the courtyard until he was out of view of the camera. David took the iPad, slid the video bar back, and watched the guy in the jacket closely again.

"That wasn't just any hand motion," David suggested.

"What was it?"

David formed his own fingers into a gun and showed her. "It was a finger gun like this. He aims it at Parker and pulls the trigger."

He rewound the video and showed her.

"You're right," Jess agreed.

They exchanged worried looks.

David felt a chill crawl down his back. "Which means he probably had a real gun hidden beneath the jacket."

FOURTEEN

At first, Richie Maylor thought the pounding he was hearing was only in his throbbing head. After all, he'd drunk himself silly last night with his buddy Manny and wasn't even sure how he'd made it back to his crappy trailer. More pounding. Was it coming from construction next door? The old guy who owned the adjacent property was building some kind of big warehouse. Richie had been hearing construction rigs lately making a lot of banging. It often started before daylight. Which was as annoying as hell, considering Richie usually slept well past noon.

Richie tried to stir but couldn't will himself to move just yet. He was lying face-first on the dirty linoleum floor in the narrow kitchen of his trailer while still wearing his jeans, cowboy boots, and jacket. He must've passed out before ever getting back to bed. His head was hurting so much, he could barely open his eyes. Had he done more than just drinking last night? He couldn't remember. Manny and his two older brothers always had their hands on the best new street drugs.

The pounding finally stopped. Thank God, Richie thought, closing his eyes to go back to sleep. Then a loud gunshot suddenly rang out behind him, exploding part of his trailer somewhere, and scared the hell out of him. He flipped over, squinted back at the door, which had swung wide-open. Daylight was now pouring inside and blinding him.

Although his vision was still blurry, Richie saw a shadow of a figure step into the trailer and move toward him. What the hell was going on? Had this guy just shot his way into his trailer? Richie tried to reach around and feel for his gun at his back. The guy met this movement with a swift kick to Richie's gut. Richie gasped for breath and curled up in pain.

"Don't bother, you idiot. Just get yourself up."

Richie immediately recognized the gravelly voice. His boss had come to pay him a visit at home—which was never a good sign. Trying to catch his breath, Richie pushed himself up from the floor. First to his knees and then gradually to his wobbly feet. His head was swirling, but he knew he had to somehow pull it together. Why was his boss here? He steadied himself with a hand on a filthy kitchen counter overrun with crumpled beer cans and paper plates covered with dried-out old food. His boss was wearing one of his usual fancy suits with no tie and expensive black dress shoes.

Richie licked his dry lips. "Hey, boss. What, uh . . . what's going on?"

"We got a big problem. The boy disappeared."

Richie tried to make sense of that. "Disapp . . . what do you mean? He's over at that children's home."

"Not anymore. He busted out of that joint last night, you moron. You should've put a bullet in him when you had the chance."

"I couldn't just shoot him in broad daylight. In front of all those other kids. Right? So I just tried to scare him enough to keep his mouth shut until I could get closer to him somehow. That place was locked up tight. I didn't know he could make a run for it."

"Well, you were wrong. He did."

The gun his boss had used to shoot open his trailer door was still clutched in his right hand. Was he there to kill him? Again, Richie wondered where he'd put his own damn gun. It was not at his back.

As if reading his mind, his boss said, "I'm not here to shoot you. Yet. I'm giving you one last chance to find that kid, and silence him. But this time, you have to put a bullet in him, Richie. I don't care if it's in broad daylight. I don't care if you're sitting in a crowded church next to your mother. You take that kid out without hesitation. You understand me?"

Richie nodded, again relieved. "I will. I promise."

His boss took a look around the trailer. "This place is absolutely disgusting. You should be ashamed to live like this."

"I'll get it cleaned up, I swear."

His boss headed back toward the door.

Richie reluctantly stopped him. "Hey, boss, I could use some help on this thing. It's a big city, you know."

His boss turned around, bunched up his face. "Then get some damn help."

"Well, it's just . . . I'm a little short on cash right now."

Richie remembered now how he'd gambled away the last $200 in his pocket last night playing cards with Manny and his two older brothers. He'd had two pairs—queens and jacks—but then Manny's brother Carlos got the flush. They damn near came to fists over it.

Staring at him with narrowed eyes, Richie's boss looked like he might have changed his mind about shooting him. Instead, he spit on the floor, took a big wad of cash out of his pocket, and tossed it onto the tattered carpet in front of Richie.

"Just so you know, Richie. When I do have you killed, it won't be with a bullet. That's too quick and easy. No, you'll die real slow. We'll take one piece of you at a time. It'll last all day. You'll get to feel every bit of it. Maybe we'll go get your mom and sister, too. It'll be a family affair."

FIFTEEN

By midmorning, David had managed to round up his boys from the Camp and gather them in the entry room of his office. He needed all the help he could get if he was going to somehow find Parker before the FBI did. That was no small task. Zegers acted like he was hitting the streets with fifty agents. David had four homeless guys on his investigative team. But these men were like his family. And he really needed his family right now.

Doc stood in one corner, arms crossed, glasses on, looking very much like the stately history teacher he had once been in life. Larue sat at the round table finishing off the glazed doughnuts Jess had brought. A young man of twenty-one with hair in cornrows, Larue wore baggy jeans and a black Miami Heat sweatshirt hoodie. Born to a crack-addicted mother, Larue had been saved from the streets by Benny two years ago. The kid was a music savant who, without having ever taken a formal lesson, had managed to get himself a steady gig playing the piano over at Pete's Dueling Piano Bar. Shifty sat next to him. A small and thin seventysomething man with wisps of bright-white hair sticking out over both ears, Shifty was a former truck driver who had been David's original tour guide when he'd first visited the Camp last year. Shifty never stopped smiling, even with half his teeth missing. Curly leaned against the wall wearing his usual denim jacket, jeans, and work boots. In his forties with a mop of brown hair, Curly was great with a tool belt and could fix just about anything. David regularly had him in the office to repair broken doors, replace wooden floor slits, build shelving units, and do other assorted projects.

David stood in the center of the room. "Doc, thanks again for driving around and picking everyone up. I appreciate you guys coming here."

"You bet," Doc said.

"Some of you have already said hello, but I wanted to more formally introduce Jess Raven." David turned and motioned toward Jess, who sat in a chair in the far corner. "Jess is a professional investigator who is here this week to assist me. I feel very fortunate to have her valuable services at such a critical time. She's already been a huge help."

All of the boys offered another friendly hello to Jess. Even though David had assured her they could help, Jess clearly did not know what to make of this misfit group. Just the same, she gave a quick but awkward wave of the hand.

David turned to Doc. "Do you have the copies of Parker's photo?"

Doc nodded and handed out copies of a profile photo David had pulled from Parker's official CPS file.

"This is Parker Barnes," David began. "He's a twelve-year-old runaway whom I helped get out of the juvenile justice center yesterday morning and took over to stay at an at-risk youth facility called the Hand-Up Home. He's a good kid who's had a really rough start to life. Tragically lost both of his parents early. Been abused in foster care. Ran away from an awful foster dad about a month ago and has been living on the streets here in Austin."

"I think I remember this kid," Larue chimed in, staring at the photo. "He's hung out with Skater some, right?"

"Correct," David replied, then added, "Which is why he got picked up for stealing purses the other night."

Larue rolled his eyes. "I keep trying to get that cat some real work so he'll stop doing that BS."

"Keep at it, Larue. Anyway, Parker ran away from the facility last night and is back out on the streets. We need to find him fast before he gets hurt. That's why you're here this morning. You're my eyes and ears out there."

"Who wants to hurt the boy, Shep?" Shifty asked.

"We're not sure yet. I should tell you, there is a bigger story at play here. The FBI thinks Parker is somehow connected to a fatal shooting that happened six nights ago over in Pease Park."

"That dead federal witness?" Curly asked.

David turned, surprised Curly knew about that.

Curly shrugged. "Someone usually brings a newspaper to the construction site. I mostly scan the sports section on breaks, but the story of the dead witness caught my attention."

"Curly is right," David said. "The dead guy was a federal witness who was set to testify. Someone made sure that didn't happen. The FBI showed up yesterday wanting to interrogate Parker, but I wouldn't allow that. He seemed too rattled. Now they're pissed at me because Parker has up and vanished. Because of that, they seem hell-bent on hunting down a scared little boy like he's some most-wanted criminal."

"Shep, you mean it's us against the FBI?" Shifty asked.

"Yes, that's what I mean."

There were some blank stares at each other across the room.

Larue said, "Well, that doesn't really seem like a fair fight."

Beside him, Shifty began to smile and snicker. "Yeah, the FBI don't stand no chance. We know these streets like the back of our hands."

Everyone laughed. David even caught Jess grinning in the corner.

"I'm counting on that, Shifty," David said. "In all seriousness, guys, I'm very concerned for Parker. I'm not sure yet how he's connected to this slaying, but Jess and I believe he's in real danger. We think he ran away from the children's home last night because someone threatened him."

David had wheeled out the TV from his office on a rolling cart. He cued up the video showing the interaction between Parker and the mystery man by the courtyard fence, pointed out where Parker was standing, and then allowed everyone to watch.

"Who is that guy?" Curly asked, stepping closer.

"We don't know yet," Jess replied. "But we think he might have had a gun hidden beneath the jacket that he flashed Parker."

"You can tell the boy's scared," Doc suggested. "Poor kid."

Jess stood and moved in next to David. "Parker called David and left a voice mail right after he ran away early this morning. Said he could no longer stay there or else someone would hurt him. That call happened at the corner of Thirty-Eighth and Lamar. That's the boy's last known location."

"He could be anywhere," David added. "I need you guys out there ASAP working the streets, talking to your friends, and getting the word out."

"You can count on us, Shep," Larue said.

"Yeah, we won't let you down," Curly concurred.

"Thanks. Keep me posted."

The guys quickly dispersed.

Alone, David huddled with Jess again.

"What do you think?" he asked her.

"Interesting guys. Do any of them even have cars?"

"Only Doc."

"Then how the hell are they going to cover the city?"

"You'd be surprised. These guys are some of the most resourceful human beings I've ever been around. And the most loyal."

"I'll take your word for it. But I don't like our chances. Zegers probably has a dozen drones canvassing Austin at this very moment. Speaking of the FBI, I want to show you something." She took David by the arm, walked him into his office and up to the window overlooking Congress Avenue.

"Gray Buick on the curb below," she said, pointing.

David peered down and noticed two guys sitting in the front seat of the sedan. He recognized them as part of Zegers's posse from yesterday. Agents Hernandez and Jeter?

"What are they doing out there?" he asked her.

"They're watching you. In case Parker tries to make contact. Just know you're probably going to have a tail everywhere you go today."

SIXTEEN

Parker carefully watched the front doors of the Walgreens, looking for his best opportunity to go inside unnoticed. He knew if he walked straight in all by himself that a store clerk might wonder what a kid his age was doing there all alone and monitor him more closely. Parker couldn't take that chance. Not now—not with what was at stake. So he waited behind a concrete column about ten paces down the sidewalk right outside the store.

His stomach was wrapped up in knots, both from not eating anything since last night and being up all night without a wink of sleep. He felt exhausted but wondered if he'd ever be able to sleep again. After bolting from the Hand-Up Home, he'd run deep into the bowels of the city, trying to create as much distance as possible away from the facility—just in case someone was out there looking for him. He had no idea how far he'd actually traveled. At first, he was counting the blocks—just to give himself some kind of bearings. But he'd stopped counting after twenty. Then he'd hid in the woods behind a new medical center until daylight.

Standing there, he could still feel a chill in his bones from wearing rain-soaked clothes during a cold night. At least the rain had finally stopped. Parker noticed a minivan pull into a parking spot close by the front doors. A mom got out, along with two boys probably around his age. The boys were pushing each other playfully like brothers often do. Parker had always wanted a brother. His dad had told him they'd planned to have another child before his mom got sick. The mom told the boys to stop goofing around, and then they trailed her toward the doors to Walgreens.

With his hoodie up over his head, Parker took that moment to hurry up and step in behind them, as if he were part of the family, and they all entered the store together. A female clerk at the front register half glanced over for a moment. The mom was telling the boys to get one snack and meet her back at the register. Parker grabbed a package of peanut butter crackers from a shelf and then moved into the back section of the store, where they offered healthcare and other assorted medicinal products. He went up and down the aisles, searching for a specific item. He finally found it on the fourth aisle with all the hair products. Electric hair clippers with batteries included. He grabbed a small box off the shelf.

Glancing up, Parker looked for video cameras. He spotted one in the corner. Positioning his back to the camera, he quickly shoved the box with the hair clippers and the peanut butter crackers into the front of his jeans beneath the hoodie and pulled the sweatshirt way down. From there, he swiftly walked toward the front of the store again, searching for the mom of the two boys. He found her kneeling in the makeup section and looking at lipsticks. Her oversize brown purse was sitting inside a red shopping basket on the floor right next to her.

Parker glanced toward the front of the store. The female clerk was busy checking out a couple of other customers. Parker had spotted another clerk three aisles behind him putting some items back on a shelf from a cart. And a third clerk was in the back corner near the pharmacy. The brothers were still over in the candy aisle. He could hear them messing with each other. Parker quickly snagged an expensive pair of sunglasses off a rack that had one of those security tags attached to it and slowly moved in behind the mom. She was still busy choosing lipsticks. He took a quick breath, let it out quietly. Then as carefully as he could without being noticed, he bent over and set the sunglasses down inside her big purse—like he was playing that Operation game and trying not to touch any of the walls and get buzzed.

He let go of the sunglasses, pulled his hand back, stood straight. At that moment, the mom turned to look up at him. He gave her a quick smile, pivoted, and walked away. His heart was racing so fast. After creating some distance, he turned around to see if the mom had noticed him with the sunglasses. She snagged the red basket with her purse inside without a second look and then walked up to the front of the store, where she found the brothers poking through gum on a front rack.

Parker eased up toward the front of the store with his eyes on a bin filled with discounted items, but he was watching the family in his peripheral vision. The brothers put giant candy bars up on the checkout counter next to their mother's makeup items from the basket. One boy had chosen Butterfinger, and the other had chosen a KIT KAT. Parker watched to see if the clerk wondered why the third son was not putting anything on the counter. But she just scanned everything, looking bored.

After paying, the mom and the boys moved toward the front doors. Parker darted in right behind them. When they passed through the security detectors, a beeping alarm suddenly went off. All three of them stopped and looked at each other. But Parker just kept on walking out the doors, his heart in his throat. Behind him, he heard the clerk ask the mom to bring the bag back over to see if she'd missed a tag or something. Parker turned the corner away from the front doors and then took off at a dead sprint.

He ran across the street to another retail strip and then hid behind the buildings near the dumpsters. Pulling out the package of peanut butter crackers, he tore off the wrapper and placed one in his mouth.

Then he tossed in two more crackers before he'd even swallowed the first. He and his dad used to stop at a convenience store after every soccer practice. He would always get peanut butter crackers and a blue Gatorade. His dad liked to get nacho cheese Doritos and a Red Bull. They would usually sit on a bench outside the convenience store, eat their snacks, and talk a little about life before going home. He missed his dad and those talks so much.

With his stomach starting to feel a little better, Parker tore open the small box that held the hair clippers. He'd never used these before but had watched his dad use a device just like this to trim up the sides and back of his hair. It didn't look too difficult. The black handheld device easily fit into his hand. Parker put the batteries into the device and then turned it on. The trimmer came to life with a gentle hum. Although he didn't have a mirror, Parker didn't think it really mattered. This didn't have to be perfect. He couldn't even remember the last time he'd had his hair cut.

Here goes nothing, he thought, then pressed the clippers to his forehead and began slowly moving them up into his hair. Big clumps of brown hair began to immediately fall onto his face. Using his free hand, he knocked the loose hair off and continued the buzz job. Several times the clippers got locked up in a thick patch of hair. There was probably a much better way to do this, but he didn't know how. So he kept pressing forward. Within a few minutes, all his shaggy brown hair was sitting in a pile beneath him. He brushed a lot of it off his clothes and then rubbed the palm of his hand up and around his now-bald head. He found a few remnants still hanging on and used the clippers to clean himself fully. He didn't know what he looked like right now—and didn't care to find out—but he felt assured that he appeared a lot different than he did yesterday. That's what mattered most.

Leaning up against the building, he finished off the rest of his peanut butter crackers. What was he going to do now? Just hide out on the streets and hope the goateed guy wouldn't find him? But what about the FBI? Would they be out looking for him, too?

Feeling cold and alone again, Parker felt tears forming in the backs of his eyes. He quickly shook his head and scolded himself. *No more crying, you big baby. Don't be such a wimp. You can do this.* He'd been trying to give himself this same pep talk ever since he'd run away last night. But it wasn't helping much. He had to think and sort out what he was going to do next. Should he make a run for another city? Stow away in another horse trailer? Maybe he could steal a car and drive for the Mexican border? Surely no one would find him in Mexico.

He'd driven a truck the one summer he was with the Bidwell family. Judd's grandpa had a ranch in south Texas with an old truck on it. He and Judd took turns behind the wheel on the wide-open land. At the time, Parker could just barely reach the pedals and had to stuff cushions under his butt to see over the dashboard and through the windshield. He gave himself whiplash for about an hour before finally getting the hang of it. Then both he and Judd had a blast all week driving that old truck up and down dirt roads and all over the ranch land. It really wasn't too difficult. But that was ranch land without any other cars around. Not the highway.

Parker sighed. He really didn't want to start all over again in a new city. He was just getting comfortable on the streets of Austin and learning how to take care of himself. He didn't want to leave. Maybe if he hid out for a week or two, it would all just go away. That's what he wanted the most. For it to all just go away, and everything to go back to normal. He grinned to himself. As if a kid his age living on the streets was normal. He thought about calling Mr. Adams again. But he knew he couldn't. Mr. Adams would probably want him to go back to the Hand-Up Home. He wouldn't understand that Parker couldn't do that. Parker had probably already gotten Mr. Adams in big trouble with the juvie judge. Mr. Adams might even be mad at him.

He took another deep breath. He would just hide. Wait it out. He could do that. The only reason anyone had found him in the first place was because the police had picked him up. So as long as he didn't do anything stupid or illegal, he should be fine. Parker remembered he'd just stolen again and kind of laughed. Okay, no more. This was the very last time.

If he kept to himself, he could hide out for months. Heck, he could hide out for years, if that's what it took. The pep talk seemed to be working.

SEVENTEEN

David and Jess left the office and began going door-to-door to all the businesses surrounding the Hand-Up Home, searching for additional security camera footage. David hoped to find something more on the mystery man who had threatened Parker in the courtyard yesterday afternoon. He presented himself as an attorney working in partnership with the FBI to find a runaway child who might be in serious danger. Part truth, part fiction. But he figured people would respond more willingly when they heard he was connected to an official authority. It worked. Most businesses were indeed helpful and allowed them access to their camera systems. In order to be efficient, they narrowed their search to the couple of hours on both ends of the fence encounter.

Unfortunately, none of the three businesses directly across the street from the courtyard fence—a Laundromat, a dry cleaner, and a veterinary clinic—had a camera that captured Parker's time with the man. So they were unable to see the man's approach and where he went right after he left. They also reviewed footage from behind the Hand-Up Home and the opposite side of its buildings, without success. David was growing frustrated. And annoyed by the sight of the gray Buick parked just up the street from his truck. The two FBI agents were not subtle in their surveillance. They were clearly okay with him knowing they were back there, waiting, watching—as if David had Parker hidden somewhere and was looking for an opportunity to slip away to reach him. Jess encouraged him to simply ignore them.

Their tedious search efforts finally paid off when they found something from a camera at a day care center directly across the street from the front doors of the Hand-Up Home. The friendly director gave them free rein inside her personal office while she had a meeting with her staff down the hallway. Jess sat at the desk behind a large computer monitor that showed the day care's full set of security cameras. David leaned in closely from behind, again finding himself distracted by Jess's fragrance.

Jess worked the video controls for a few minutes before David spotted something.

"There," David said, pointing at the computer screen. "That's him, right?"

"Same goatee, jean jacket, jeans, and boots."

Jess rewound the video, and they watched again. At exactly 3:37 p.m., according to the time log on the video, the same man who'd approached Parker had come around the corner of the sidewalk near the front of the Hand-Up Home.

"This is a much better shot of him than the inner courtyard video," Jess said.

"Are you able to zoom in even closer?"

Jess paused the video, enhanced the guy's face until it began to blur on the screen.

"I'd guess midtwenties," Jess said.

"Rough-looking guy. Let's see how far we can track him."

Jess pressed "Play" again. The guy quickly walked to a black Ford truck that was jacked up with big mud tires. Because it was parked parallel to the curb, David couldn't get a clear look at the license plate. The guy climbed into the vehicle, lit up a cigarette, and then pulled away.

"Damn, no plates."

Jess began rewinding the video. "Maybe we can get a shot of when he arrived."

They discovered the guy had pulled up in his truck around two thirty that afternoon. But the angle toward the back bumper of the vehicle was completely blocked by other parked cars. Still no good license plate shot. At that point, the guy with the goatee had gotten out of his truck, stared over toward the front of the Hand-Up Home, lit a cigarette, and puffed while just standing there for about ten minutes.

David watched him closely. Who was this guy? Was his encounter with Parker random? Was he just some creep? Or was he the reason the boy had run away from the home this morning? Was he the guy Parker had said was going to *hurt him bad* in the voice mail?

The man finally walked away from his truck and began strolling to his left until he was completely out of camera view.

Jess glanced up at him. "What do you think?"

"Not much to go by."

Jess turned back to the screen. "What about all of those stickers he has on the back window?"

David leaned in again. "Can you enhance that shot?"

Jess pulled up a shot of the truck's dirty back window. There were about a dozen faded stickers covering the bottom border. Random skulls and crossbones. Half-naked ladies. Coors. Budweiser. Jack Daniel's. Freddy's Salvage. Little River Dragway. The Burping Goat. Remington firearms. David was already searching on his phone.

"Freddy's Salvage is a local junkyard," he said.

Jess was also on her phone. "Little River Dragway is a racetrack about an hour north of here."

David studied the sticker for the Burping Goat, which showed a cartoon goat chugging a mug of beer. He typed into his phone. "The Burping Goat looks like a local bar."

"The bar and the junkyard are worth checking out," Jess suggested. "Maybe we can find someone who recognizes this guy."

"Worth a shot."

"Let's split up. I'll head to the bar. You and your FBI pals can take the junkyard."

She gave him a playful smile. He rolled his eyes.

"Call me if you find something," he said.

EIGHTEEN

Using her maps app, Jess followed directions for about fifteen minutes until she pulled into a run-down retail strip in a seedy part of the city with a convenience store on one end, a paint store in the middle, and the Burping Goat bar at the opposite end. The same logo with a goat chugging a beer was in neon lights above the front door. Because it was midday, the bar was currently closed. No vehicles were parked outside, either. A faded sticker on a window said the bar opened at three. She pulled on the red wooden front doors but found them locked. Then she peered through the filthy windows to see if she could spot anyone inside. She could hardly see anything because the glass panes were covered in so much dirt and grime. But she spotted a collection of pool tables with a long bar in the back. She gave several firm knocks on the front door, waited, but got no response.

Circling around to the back of the building, Jess spotted four overflowing metal dumpsters. Boxes and trash bags were spilling out the top of each one. It smelled like a mix of cigarettes, alcohol, and vomit. This was not exactly a high-end establishment. She found an older Dodge Ram truck parked directly behind the bar. Maybe someone was here. As she approached the back door to the bar, it swung open. A young guy in his early twenties with a thick mustache and wearing faded jeans and a pearl-snap shirt unbuttoned to his stomach appeared with two trash bags in his fists. The guy was tan and muscular and looked like he should be doing ads for a Western magazine.

"Hi there," Jess said with a friendly smile. He paused, took a good long look at her. "Well, hello yourself."

"You work here?"

"Yep." He stepped past her to one of the dumpsters and swung both trash bags high up on top of a mountain of other bags. Turning back, he wiped his hands on his jeans. "You need something?"

"I'm looking for someone."

He grinned. "I hope that someone is a charming cowboy like me."

She matched his grin, willing to be flirty. "Not today."

"Well, that's a damn shame."

She introduced herself. He said his name was Cody.

"Who're you looking for, Jess?"

She held up her phone to show him a close-up of the guy with the goatee standing beside his black truck. "You recognize this guy? I think he might come around here."

The bartender studied the photo. "Yeah, I recognize him. That's Richie."

"Do you know his last name?"

He shook his head. "Nah, sorry. I don't think I've ever caught it. He always pays in cash. But you're right; he's here all the time. Although now that I think about it, I haven't seen him here all week. Probably in jail or something."

"Why do you say that?"

Cody shrugged. "The guy is kind of a troublemaker. I've had to break up a couple of fights. Why're you looking for him?"

"I'm an investigator trying to help a troubled child. We think Richie is important to the case. When was the last time you saw him?"

Cody twisted up his mouth. "Probably Sunday night. I only remember because the Cowboys were playing the Giants. The bar was crowded. And Richie was saying how he was going to buy a round of drinks for everyone whenever he got back."

"Got back from where?"

"Hell if I know. He left early and never came back."

Jess felt her adrenaline kick into gear. Sunday was six days ago. The same night when Max Legley, the federal witness, was shot dead in the city park.

"How often did Richie buy drinks for everyone?"

"Never. But he said he was about to get paid. None of us took him seriously."

Get paid? Could someone have hired the guy to kill Legley?

"Any idea how I might find Richie?" she asked.

"Not really. Sorry. Maybe come back tonight? See if he shows up?"

"Okay, thanks. I really appreciate your help."

"Anytime. If you do come back tonight, drinks are on me."

She smiled. "I'll think about it."

Cody's face tightened up a bit. "Hey, but seriously, be careful with Richie. I'm not usually one to talk badly of people, but that guy is trouble. I've learned to spot the bad seeds. And that guy has *bad* written all over him. I just don't want to see someone as beautiful as you getting hurt."

NINETEEN

David pulled his truck up to a small portable building with a cheap sign out front that said "Freddy's Salvage" and a tag below that read "Do the Picking to Keep Your Car Ticking." Behind the dingy building was a dirt field full of heaps of beat-up old cars that looked like they had all been picked apart. Some were missing bumpers; others, doors, tires, and so forth. In the middle of the dusty rows, he spotted someone operating a huge forklift and digging a car out of one of the piles. Could that be the guy with the goatee? David had wondered why the mystery man would have a sticker of a junkyard on his truck unless he worked there or something. Although there didn't seem to be much discrimination in his choice of window stickers. David squinted and then shook his head. The guy on the forklift was older, with a ponytail poking out the back of a ball cap.

Still, David wanted to be on guard in case the guy popped out somewhere and didn't like seeing someone asking questions about him. Getting out, David peered behind him and watched the gray Buick settle onto the side of the road about fifty yards away. He fought the urge to flip them the bird. Walking up to the front door of the portable building, David couldn't tell if it was an actual office or a home residence. He knocked. A few seconds later, a man with a long gray beard and blue overalls opened the door. He had on the thickest glasses David had ever seen. And he still seemed to be squinting through them at him.

"Well, hello, can I help you?"

"Are you Freddy?"

"Yes, sir, Freddy Lenard. At your service."

"My name is David Adams. I'm an attorney. I'm hoping you can help me find someone, Mr. Lenard."

"Please, call me Freddy."

"Okay, Freddy." David held up a still shot on his phone of the goateed guy. "Any chance you recognize this man?"

Freddy's eyes narrowed in on the image. "Well, sure, that's Richie Maylor. He used to work for me."

David made a quick mental note of the name. That was a big help already. "But he no longer works here?"

"No, I'm afraid not. Things didn't work out."

"Any idea how I might find Mr. Maylor?"

"Well, come on inside. Let me see what I can do."

Freddy held the door open and allowed David into the building. It was indeed an office. Everything was nice and neat, which David had not expected when he'd approached the dirty building. Two desks were on the right side of the room, with bookshelves and file cabinets behind them. There was a long folding table with metal folding chairs around it in the middle of the room. Then on the opposite end was a kitchen with a refrigerator.

Freddy made his way around one of the desks and sat in a brown leather chair. "Please, have a seat, Mr. Adams. Why are you looking for Richie?"

David sat in a comfortable chair in front of the desk. "Well, sir, I'm working on an important case that involves him."

Freddy looked up. "Oh boy. What has that boy gone and done now?"

"I'm not sure yet. I just need to find him."

"Well, I know I have his contact info in a file." He spun around in his chair and began pulling drawers out of a cabinet.

"How long did Richie work for you?" David asked.

"Not too long. A couple of months."

"Why is he no longer working here?"

"Well, Richie had trouble showing up on time. And sometimes he wouldn't show up at all."

"So you fired him?"

"Well, I'm afraid so. I wanted to give that boy a chance. Not too many are willing to hire ex-cons, but I like to give people second chances, you know. And sometimes third chances. For heaven's sake, the good Lord has given me a lot of second and third chances."

"So Richie was incarcerated?"

"Yes, sir."

"Do you know what for?"

"I'm not too sure. He never really talked about it. I didn't ask. Didn't want him to feel like I was judging him."

"What else can you tell me about him?"

Freddy continued to search his file cabinet. "Not too much. He kind of kept to himself most of the time. When he actually showed up, he did good work. He seemed to have a knack for driving the forklift. Although he'd get mad at it here and there and cuss up a storm. I had to get on him a few times about that. I got grandkids that come around the property. I don't need them hearing the Lord's name taken in vain." Freddy seemed to have finally found what he was looking for. "Here we go."

Spinning around in the chair, he put a manila folder on the desk and opened it. David spotted the name *Richard Maylor* written on the tab. Inside, Freddy found an employment form that Richie had filled out.

"This ought to do," Freddy said, handing it to David.

The form listed Richie's phone number and home address. David was really getting somewhere now. "Mind if I take a picture of this?"

"Help yourself."

David snapped a photo, immediately texted it to Jess.

"I really do hope everything is okay with that boy," Freddy said. "I know Richie has a lot of issues. From what I gathered, he hasn't had the easiest of lives. But I could see some good in him. If only given the right kind of shepherding and guidance, that boy can still make something of his life."

David didn't have the heart to tell Freddy that it appeared Richie Maylor was up to no good. What exactly, he still didn't know. But threatening to shoot a twelve-year-old boy was not a positive sign.

"I really appreciate this, Freddy. You've been a big help."

"You bet. Good luck."

When he stepped outside the building, David got a return text from Jess.

Meet you there. I've got interesting news.

TWENTY

Richie stood in the filthy kitchen of a mobile home on cinder blocks that belonged to Manny's oldest brother, Carlos, who was leaning against a counter, drinking from a bottle of Coors Light. Carlos was in his early thirties, with thick shoulders that popped out of a white tank top. Tattoos of different women's faces covered both of his muscular arms. Manny sat in a metal folding chair by a small kitchen table. He was much smaller than his oldest brother, but that hadn't stopped him from being one of the best fighters Richie had ever seen. They'd been friends since middle school. Manny had saved his ass more times than he could count. They did everything together, including their time in lockup. Manny wore a white T-shirt and dirty jeans with cowboy boots and had a pencil-thin black mustache. He'd never been able to grow much facial hair.

Manny's other brother, Hector, was also there. Hector was slightly overweight, with a thick black beard. Although he was the quietest of the brothers, Hector was probably the meanest. Growing up, Richie had watched him torture small animals just for kicks. Hector went to prison at eighteen for shoving an elderly woman to the concrete while stealing her purse right outside a grocery store. He was high as a kite that day. The old woman broke several ribs, her collarbone, and hip, and barely survived the fall. Hector didn't seem to care—the guy just lacked the empathy gene. They were a motley crew, but they always looked after Richie like he was family.

"What kid?" Carlos asked.

Richie was explaining his situation with Parker Barnes and his need for help in finding the boy. "Just some stupid kid that saw something he shouldn't have. And now I need to find him and shut him up."

"Whatcha mean, shut him up?" Hector said.

"What do you think I mean?"

"You want us to kill a kid, bro?" Manny asked him.

Even though they were best friends, Richie had not shared with Manny any details about this job for his boss. Mainly because his boss had told him to keep his mouth shut.

"You don't have to kill him," Richie insisted. "Just help me find him."

"I don't have a problem killing some kid," Hector mentioned.

"What's in it for us?" Carlos asked, crossing his massive arms. "We ain't driving around town looking for some kid for you for nothing."

"I know that," Richie replied. "I got you covered."

Richie pulled out the wad of cash his boss had given him earlier. This immediately got the brothers' full attention.

"Where the hell did you get that?" Manny asked.

"Yeah, man," Hector said, frowning. "You said you were completely tapped out last night."

"Chill, bro. I got it this morning."

"How much?" Carlos asked, eyeballing the wad.

The wad was one-hundred-dollar bills. Richie quickly counted out three stacks of $500 on the counter. His boss had given him $3,000. He kept the rest of the cash in his boot, planning to save that for himself. Unless Manny and his brothers needed more coercing.

"Five hundred for each of you. Not bad for one day's work."

"Hell yeah," Manny said, perking up.

Carlos eyeballed Richie. "Where did you get that kind of money, Richie?"

"Why does it matter? The money is good."

"Where's the rest of it?" Carlos said.

"That's all I've got," Richie lied.

For a second, Richie wondered if Carlos was going to shake him down. If the big brother found the money in his boot, Richie was going to get a major beating. Carlos had kicked his ass plenty of times. Fortunately, Carlos let the moment pass.

"All right, I'm in," Hector said, standing up and grabbing his stack off the counter. "I don't care who the job is for. I got bills to pay."

"Same," chimed in Manny, grabbing his stack.

Richie turned to Carlos, who still seemed skeptical. "Well?"

Carlos finally picked up his money. "You know I'm going to beat the hell out of you if this thing goes south."

"It won't," Richie reassured him. "All I need you to do is help me find this kid. That's it, Carlos. I'll take care of the rest. I swear."

Carlos finally seemed satisfied. "All right."

Richie smiled. "Okay, let's go."

TWENTY-ONE

Zegers hopped out of Farley's black Tahoe in front of a half-finished midtown four-story office building that had apparently been abandoned last year when the company behind the project went bankrupt. Farley joined him on the sidewalk outside the building, which sat next to several other completed office buildings. The structure of the office building was in place but with nothing finished inside. It was just drab concrete, columns, loose wires, and cables. But according to his team, the building was known to be a place where runaway teens liked to hide out because it was close to UT's campus. A lot of these homeless kids hung around the university since they were at least among similar-age people. His team had been actively hunting places just like this in hopes of finding the boy. So far, nothing.

Zegers was frustrated on multiple levels. A crappy beginning of his day had only gotten worse upon seeing Jess Raven—a source of recent humiliation for him. On his date with Jess a few months ago, Zegers had foolishly texted a couple of his buddies during the date, while she was in the restroom, to brag on how he was about to get very lucky. Then she'd skipped out on him with a feigned illness and didn't return any of his phone calls. He would've lied to his friends about the whole thing if he and Jess hadn't shared common social circles. So he was stuck wearing egg on his face. Needless to say, his buddies hadn't let him live it down ever since. They kept texting him: You getting lucky today, Harry? LOL.

Four other agents stepped out of the building and met them on the sidewalk. They had arrived a few minutes before Zegers and Farley. All of them wore civilian clothes: sweatshirts, windbreakers, jeans, khakis. Zegers had instructed his whole team to dress casual so they wouldn't stand out on the streets. Instead of his usual snazzy sport coat, Zegers wore a dark-blue Auburn Tigers hoodie, jeans, and tennis shoes.

"Anything?" Zegers asked Norton, head of this group of agents.

"The building is definitely a makeshift homeless shelter."

"What do we have in there?" Zegers asked.

"Probably fifty or so," Norton replied. "Mostly on the second floor. But they are scattered throughout the building. Elevator doesn't work, of course. We'll have to take the stairs up in the middle."

"Everyone got his photo?" Zegers said.

They all held up their phones showing the booking photo of Parker Barnes that Zegers had taken from the juvenile justice center. Parker wore the orange jumpsuit with his pale face looking sullen and his shaggy brown hair hanging down over his ears.

"All right, let's see if we can find him in there."

Zegers followed his agents across the parking lot toward the building. So far, they'd had few leads, even though Zegers had managed to pull in a dozen agents to aid in the search. The fact that the US Attorney's Office was bringing a lot of additional heat to the situation helped Zegers get the resources he needed. While pissed that the kid was missing, Mark Anderson was also as hopeful as ever that the boy was the key to getting his trial back on track. According to Anderson, Parker Barnes would not have run away if he didn't know what happened to their dead witness. They just had to find him. As if to annoy Zegers, the federal prosecutor was even driving around town himself in his fancy Mercedes, looking for the boy. Zegers had checked in with Agents Jeter and Hernandez, who had been monitoring David Adams all day, but they had nothing much to show for it. They said the attorney drove a few places, but there had been no hints that he knew where the boy might be hiding.

Zegers followed his agents into the wide-open first floor of the building. Half of the exterior walls had not been finished, so a chilly breeze pushed through the structure. Because of the concrete, it felt even colder to him inside the building than outside. There was trash strewn all over the place on the first level, but no sign of any people. They hit the building stairwell in the middle and traveled up to the second floor.

Zegers immediately spotted a large group of the homeless gathered in the farthest corner of the building away from the front. They probably chose the second level because they were more hidden from the street, and the wind was not quite as bad up here. Zegers noticed a huge collection of makeshift tents, some covered in blankets, with more trash everywhere. There were also several campfires going at the moment. Zegers did a quick count and guessed there were indeed around fifty people, many sleeping on the hard concrete with dirty blankets. Some had sleeping bags; others sat in camping chairs. There was also a lot of smoking and drinking, with other assorted drug paraphernalia being passed around.

"Be cool, boys," Zegers instructed his team. "Don't spook anyone."

As they approached the group, Zegers and his crew drew suspicious stares. Even though they weren't dressed in police uniforms, it was clear they didn't belong here. A few guys immediately got up from the floor and started leaving, as if the sign of any outsiders was enough for them to split. But most of the group held steady while closely watching Zegers and his crew. His agents began flashing the photo of Parker around, asking if anyone had seen the kid and mentioning him by name. They got mostly blank stares and shakes of the head. Some couldn't respond at all; they were so high at the moment. Zegers didn't see a lot of young faces in this group of people. Where were the runaway teens?

Farley came back over to Zegers. "One of the guys told me the kids are upstairs on the third floor."

"Then let's go up," Zegers said.

Farley summoned the others, and they all hit the stairwell again. Entering the third floor, Zegers noticed a collection of about twelve street teens all huddled in the far corner. This group was much more skittish than the downstairs group. Upon spotting the group of men approaching, the teenagers immediately began gathering their things to get out of there.

Norton jumped in to stop them. "Hey, stop! FBI! Everyone stay put."

Zegers cursed at that foolish move. It was like lighting a match near a gas leak. Now the group of kids was really on the run, making mad dashes for exits. Zegers and his crew stepped right into the middle of the chaos, grabbing kids to look at them as they all tried to scramble to get away. Zegers frantically searched the dirty faces for any signs of Parker Barnes. Most of these boys looked older than Parker. There were also a few girls. But none of them stayed still long enough to really examine them. Zegers had Parker's booking photo up on his own phone. He kept bouncing his eyes back and forth between the photo and the kids before they were able to pull away from him. It was all happening so fast that he couldn't be sure if he missed someone. Within seconds, the floor was completely empty of kids, leaving only the agents standing there and staring at each other.

"Nice work," Zegers scolded Norton.

"What the hell was I supposed to do? They were all about to bolt."

"They were walking away, not running," Farley said. "Until you opened your big mouth."

"Just drop it," Zegers interjected. "Anyone see anything?"

They all shook their heads.

"What about you, boss?" Farley asked.

"No, I don't think the kid was here."

TWENTY-TWO

Richie was driving around central Austin in his truck with Manny sitting in the seat next to him when a text suddenly popped up on his cell phone. He snagged it from a cupholder, stared at the urgent message, and then nearly rear-ended a car in front of him before slamming on the brakes just in time to avoid the collision.

"What the hell, bro?" Manny said. "Trying to get us killed?"

Richie turned to look at Manny. "We got eyes on the boy!"

"Where?"

"Four blocks from here," Richie said, whipping his steering wheel to the left and stomping on the gas.

The truck tires squealed on the pavement as he did a swift U-turn into the next lane, causing several cars coming from the opposite direction to swerve and slam on brakes. The truck rapidly accelerated. With his left hand clutched on the steering wheel, Richie set his right hand down on top of his gun on the seat next to him.

It was time to end this right now.

TWENTY-THREE

Along with several other boys, Parker ran as fast as he could down the sidewalk away from the abandoned office building where he'd been hiding out the past couple of hours. His heart was racing so fast his chest hurt. The FBI? Parker couldn't believe it. How did they know he'd be there in that building? How did they find him so fast? He thought he'd be safe just hanging out there for a while. He'd been in the building twice before with Skater, who seemed to know everyone out on the streets. None of the other kids had asked him any questions—which was not unusual. Most guys just kept to themselves. Which was what he'd wanted. Although one nice guy had come over to him in the corner and offered to share some bread and peanut butter. Everything was going well until those FBI men had unexpectedly showed up, flashing his photo to everyone.

Parker nearly tripped over a curb just thinking about it again. One of the FBI men had grabbed him by the collar before he could get away. It had nearly choked him and taken him off his feet before he hit the concrete square on his butt. Then the man had flipped Parker over and stared him right in the face. The man had looked back and forth between Parker and the photo on his phone several times. Parker thought it was over—that he'd been busted. But the FBI man suddenly let him go and moved on to the next kid. Had the man really not recognized he was the same kid in the photo? Had cutting off all his hair really worked that well?

Parker didn't know for sure, but he was glad to get the hell out of there with the others. But where would he go next? The FBI had found him so quickly. Two older runaway boys were running up ahead of him. One of them was the nice guy who had offered Parker the bread and peanut butter. Parker was following that guy but not sure what he was doing. He was just running on adrenaline at the moment. Everyone had scrambled in all different directions. Finally, after a few more blocks, the boys in front stopped running and started walking. Parker did the same but hung back a bit. Peering behind him, Parker could still see the abandoned office building in the distance. He'd gotten away. But would he ever get that lucky again?

"Hey, kid, come here."

Parker turned back around to see the boy with the peanut butter inviting him to join them up on the sidewalk. He was probably sixteen or so, with dirty blond hair hanging around his shoulders. He had tattoos of spiderwebs all over his hands. The other kid may have been older than sixteen. He had black hair that was completely shaved on both sides of his head. Parker could see tattoos on this guy's neck of fire-breathing dragons. A lot of the runaways on the streets had tattoos. Parker wondered if he'd end up with a lot of tattoos one day—assuming he didn't get picked up by the FBI and hauled off to rot in prison.

Parker hesitantly walked up to them.

"You the kid in that photo?" the blond guy asked Parker.

Parker shook his head. "Nope."

"Yeah, you are," the other guy said. "Why they looking for you?"

"That's not me in the photo," Parker insisted. "That kid had long hair. I don't." Parker pulled his hood off to show his shaved head.

"That's true," admitted the blond guy. "Still, you kind of look like him."

"I said I'm not. So drop it."

"Okay, tough guy," the dragon-tattoo kid said with a smirk.

Both teenagers squinted at him, as if they were trying to figure out whether they believed him—or if they cared. But the fact that they were even wondering about it really made Parker feel uncomfortable. How was he going to hide out for several more weeks if the FBI was showing his photo to everyone out on the streets? He might not last the day. He could cut his hair, but he couldn't change his whole face.

He was starting to feel scared again. But that feeling paled in comparison to how he felt just two seconds later when a black truck suddenly pulled to a stop on the street right next to them. Parker glanced over. The driver's window was down, and two guys were sitting in the front of the truck, staring at him. Parker made direct eye contact with the driver and felt his heart drop to the concrete. He'd never forget the face of the man from the park.

For a second, the guy with the goatee just stared at him with narrowed eyes, as if trying to make sure Parker was the same kid. Probably because of the hair. Parker hoped if he just stayed still and acted cool, the guy would assume he wasn't the one they were looking for. Then Parker saw the recognition settle in on the man's face. The guy immediately opened his door, jumped out of the truck, and Parker spotted the gun clutched in the guy's right hand.

"What the hell?" said one of the runaways.

"He's got a gun!" said the other kid. "Let's go!"

The two boys took off. Parker spun around, began running in the opposite direction. Then he realized he was headed right back toward the abandoned office building where he'd just escaped the FBI. Those men could still be out looking for him. So he darted left at the next street corner, cut in behind more office buildings. He had no idea where he was going but knew he couldn't stay out in the open for too long. The goateed guy would probably shoot him.

After passing by the first office building, Parker noticed a parking garage beneath the second building. A car was pulling out from behind an electronic bar gate. Parker glanced behind him and spotted the goateed man and the other guy racing around the street corner and hustling down the sidewalk toward him.

In a split second, Parker made the decision to run inside the underground parking garage, hoping he might be able to win a game of hide-and-seek. A sign on a column said the garage had two levels. Entering, Parker found it filled with cars. Should he find a quick hiding place and hope the guys chasing him brushed right past? Or should he go deep into the garage to get himself lost? Everything within Parker screamed at him to keep running deeper and deeper into the garage. But he knew that was driven by fear. His gut instinct told him to hide right now. The men would never expect it. But did he have the balls to do it?

Gritting his teeth, Parker peeled off behind a gray Lexus SUV only ten cars down the first row. He dropped to the concrete and then scooted behind the back wheels against the concrete wall. He put his hand over his mouth to try to hide how hard he was breathing. He inched down even closer to the floor so he could see beneath the vehicle. Then he stopped breathing altogether. The two guys were inside the garage with him. He spotted their shoes and boots. They paused just three cars up from his hiding spot.

"You see anything?" one guy said.

Parker thought it was the goateed man. He recognized his voice.

"No, but he definitely ran in here."

"Come on!"

As the men moved closer to his spot, Parker curled up as tight as possible and prayed he was invisible. Even though he needed to catch his breath in the worst way, he still held it so he wouldn't make a single sound. The guys were directly in front of the Lexus now. They paused again. Parker nearly screamed. Then they moved past him. And they kept moving more quickly down the row of cars. Parker finally breathed again. But he knew there was no time to waste. When the guys reached the bottom level without finding him, they would quickly come back up on another search.

Parker eased around the Lexus on his hands and knees until he was near the front tire. He slowly peeked out. The men were nearly to the end of the first level where it made a turn and went to the next level down. The guy with the goatee briefly glanced back up the ramp. Parker darted back. Had he been spotted? If so, the guy hadn't said anything. Parker eased back out to look again. The men were making the turn down to the next level.

Parker waited until they were fully out of view. And then he scooted around the front bumper of the Lexus. He hung close to the other vehicles so as to not expose himself until he was all the way back to the entrance to the parking garage. Before running out, he took a good long look around outside to make sure there wasn't anyone else out there who might be searching for him. There were a couple of people on the sidewalks and a few others getting in and out of cars parked along the street. But none of them seemed to be on the lookout for anyone.

Taking another deep breath, Parker ran out of the parking garage. He hit the sidewalk at full speed and just kept running. Again, he had no idea where he was going or when to stop.

But Parker knew one thing for sure.

He couldn't do this alone. He needed help.

TWENTY-FOUR

David parked behind Jess's black Ford Explorer on the side of a dusty pothole-filled country road. A desolate plot of land that hosted a beat-up old RV trailer sat in front of him. The home of Richie Maylor, according to the employment form David had gotten from Freddy's Salvage. It was out in the middle of nowhere. David had spotted only a couple of other residences for the past mile. Most were run-down trailers like this one, which looked like it hadn't been moved in a really long time. Tall grass was growing up all around it. It was slightly off-balance and kind of sagged to the left. There was one vehicle parked out front, although he was certain it hadn't been driven in ages. The old truck was rusted out, had two front tires missing, and had been completely enveloped in uncut grass and weeds. There were a couple of plastic lawn chairs sitting outside the trailer. A huge collection of what he guessed were empty beer cans covered the dirt ground around the chairs. There were a couple of rusted red barrels nearby. Other assorted trash and junk was scattered here and there. The place was a real dump.

Getting out, David turned and watched as the gray Buick with the two FBI agents pulled to the side of the road about fifty yards back. He rolled his eyes and then walked over to where Jess was waiting for him near the front of her vehicle.

"Still back there, huh?" Jess said, peering around him at the Buick.

"Yeah. Our tax dollars at work." He stared at the trailer. "Is anyone home?"

"I haven't seen anyone. But I just got here."

"You said you had interesting news."

"Yes, I spoke with a bartender at the Burping Goat. He knew Richie Maylor—although he didn't know his last name. He said Maylor was at the bar almost every night. But he hadn't seen him since this past Sunday. He said Maylor left early but told everyone he was about to get paid and was going to buy a round of drinks for everyone when he got back later that night. But he never came back."

David thought about the timeline. "Sunday night was when Max Legley was shot."

"Right. Hard to believe that's a coincidence. I just ran a background check on Maylor. He did eighteen months for violent assault."

"So he fits the bill. You think Rick Kingston hired him to take out his business partner before he testified against him?"

"Maybe. Although I did a Google search matching up Maylor's name with both Kingston and Legley and found nothing connecting them online. Not much showed up on Maylor at all. No social media. No apparent involvement in any clubs or organizations. No comments or posts on any online forums. At least under his real name."

"So if it was Kingston, how did he find Maylor?"

"No clue. But the bigger question for me right now is how did Richie Maylor know that Parker was at the Hand-Up Home?"

"Right. Because he showed up right after I checked the kid into the facility."

Jess looked toward the trailer. "Shall we go see if he's home and ask him?"

"If the guy is a potential killer, do you really think we should be knocking on his front door right now?"

"Don't worry, I'll protect you."

"How?"

Jess pulled up the front of her shirt enough to show him a waistband holster holding a gun. "In my line of work, you have to be prepared for anything. Just comes with the territory."

"Great. Let's have an old-fashioned shoot-out."

"We'll be fine; don't worry. Plus, we have your pals in the Buick over there as backup if things get really nuts."

"Harry Zegers would probably love to hear that I got shot."

But with Parker in danger, David knew they needed to be bold right now. They couldn't waste any time. So he led the way up the dirt driveway to the trailer.

Two small windows were in front. Jess did a quick peek in both but shook her head like she didn't see anything. Swallowing, David knocked. From the corner of his eye, he noticed Jess put her hand inside her jacket near her waist. No one answered the door. He looked down toward the door handle and noticed it wasn't there. Instead, there was a big hole in the door with chunks of fiberglass material missing all around it.

"Looks like someone busted up the door."

Jess studied it. "That's actually a gunshot."

David sighed. "This just keeps getting better and better. Maybe he's dead in there."

"Only one way to find out." Jess pulled slightly at the door. It was open. "Let's have a look around inside."

"What about the feds?"

"What are they going to do? Arrest us?"

"You were the kid that got everyone else detention, weren't you?"

She smiled, winked at him. "I promise to be quick."

David pulled the door open and poked his head inside. "Hello? Anyone home?"

No answer. No sounds from anywhere in the trailer. They both stepped fully inside. The smell of the place nearly made him gag. A mix of beer, marijuana, old food, and sweaty laundry. To their right was a small sitting area with a tiny couch and chair. Both furniture items were dated and looked dirty and stained. To their left was a small kitchen. Beyond that was a bathroom and a bedroom.

"This guy is a slob," Jess said.

"Wonder if he's even been here this week."

Jess wandered into the kitchen. She rummaged through a few fast-food bags sitting on the counter and held up a receipt. "He's been here. This is from last night."

David began searching around the living room. There was a stack of magazines sitting in the chair. Most were about cars and hunting. A few nudie mags. Clothes were strewn all about. There were dirty ashtrays and empty beer cans everywhere.

Thankfully, there were no dead bodies.

"This is definitely his place," Jess said from the kitchen. "Maylor's name is on all of these unopened bills."

David joined her in the kitchen. Dirty dishes and dozens of take-out food containers and sacks covered nearly every square inch of counter space. He opened the small refrigerator and found a couple of dishes inside with what looked like mold growing on them along with two six-packs of Coors Light. David moved into the tiny bedroom. It was basically just a queen-size mattress on the floor. There wasn't much room for anything other than sleeping. The bed was unmade. He found a pile of empty cigarette cartons sitting next to an overflowing ashtray. The smoke smell was overwhelming and made him start coughing up a fit. When he stopped, he heard a car door slam right outside the trailer.

"We've got company," Jess announced.

David hurried back through the kitchen. Jess was peering out a front window.

"Who is it?" David asked.

"Not Maylor. Some chick."

David leaned in beside Jess, stared out the dirty window. A woman in her twenties had just stepped out of a dusty black Hyundai. She had

curly bleached-blonde hair and an ample bosom that she gladly show-
cased beneath a tight pink T-shirt that looked like it had exploded with
glitter. She also had a serious frown on her face.

"She doesn't look too happy," David mentioned.

"You'd better let me handle this."

Jess moved to the door and opened it. David watched from the
window. The sight of Jess standing in the door of the trailer made the
woman pause a few feet away.

"Who the hell are you?" she said to Jess.

"Hey, have you seen Richie?" Jess casually asked.

"I'll ask you the same damn thing. Are you his latest cheat?"

The woman looked like she wanted to charge and attack Jess. David
wondered if Jess was going to have to pull out her handgun after all.

"Uh, no," Jess replied. "I'm just looking for Richie."

"Why? He's already got a girlfriend."

"I'm guessing that would be you."

"You're damn right, honey."

"Look, I'm not here to cause you any grief. I'm only here on business. Do you know where I can find Richie?"

"Hell if I know. I haven't seen him all week. That ass won't answer
his phone. I swear he's out there cheating again. If I catch him, he's a
dead man."

"How long have you and Richie been dating?"

"Six months."

"Richie ever mention someone named Rick Kingston?"

"No. Who is that?"

"What about Max Legley?"

She shook her head. "Don't know that name, either. Who are you
again? You said you was here on business. But Richie ain't even got a job
right now. Other than some work he's doing for that one guy."

David stepped into the doorway with Jess. "What one guy?"

The woman looked over to David. "Who are you?"

"I'm with her," David said, nodding at Jess. "You said Richie was working for a guy. Who?"

She shrugged. "I don't know him."

"Do you know his name?" David asked.

Her face bunched up. "Why should I talk to you? As a matter of fact, why the hell are you guys inside Richie's trailer? That's trespassing. I should call the cops on you right now."

"The cops are already here, ma'am," David replied, thinking fast.

"Where?" the woman asked.

"You see that Buick parked on the road over there? That's the FBI. Those two federal agents are working with us. So this can go two ways for you. You can tell us what you know, and you'll be free to go. Otherwise, we might have to bring you down to FBI headquarters for more questioning."

She glanced over at the Buick. "You're lying. I don't believe you."

"Then go ask to see their IDs."

She studied David a moment, calling his bluff.

But David just crossed his arms. "Go on, we'll wait here."

"Fine, I will," the woman huffed.

She turned and stomped up the dirt driveway toward the street.

"You think this will work?" Jess whispered to him.

"I have no idea. But worth a try."

David watched as the woman reached the Buick a few seconds later. Looking confused, the FBI agent on the driver's side rolled down the window. The woman said something and then pointed over toward David and Jess. In response, the agent pulled out his wallet and showed her his identification. Examining it, the woman stiffened a bit. She said another quick word to the agent and then turned to walk back. David could see a clear change in her facial demeanor. The scowl had been replaced by wide-eyed worry.

"I think it worked," David said. "Come on."

David stepped out of the trailer, Jess behind him, and they met the woman at the foot of the dirt driveway.

"Well?" David asked.

"Look, I'm real sorry I yelled at you," the woman said, a complete change in her tone. "I'm just on edge. I'm worried about Richie. Is he in trouble with the FBI or something?"

"Not yet," Jess said, stepping in closer to the woman. She put a comforting hand on the woman's arm. "But it's important for you to tell us the truth. For Richie's sake. Do you know the name of the guy Richie has been doing work for?"

"No, he just said he had to do a job for someone he called Dilly. That's all."

David and Jess shared a glance. That name didn't register anything. "You ever heard that name before?" David asked the woman.

"Nope. But Richie don't ever tell me much."

"He mention anything else about what this job entailed?" Jess asked her.

She shook her head. "No, but he promised me he was going to buy me a diamond necklace when he finished it. So I guess he was going to make some good money. Unless he was lying to me again. You never know with Richie."

"When did he tell you this?"

"Sunday. When we were fishing."

"And you haven't seen him since Sunday?"

"No. Doesn't make any sense. He's disappeared on me before. But not this long."

"Thank you for your help," Jess said.

"Can I go now?"

"Yes," Jess replied.

They watched as the woman got back into her Hyundai and drove away.

Jess turned to him. "You're a genius."

"We make a good team. But who is Dilly?"

"I don't know. Let's go find out."

TWENTY-FIVE

Zegers hit ninety on the speedometer in his Jeep Wrangler as he raced up US 183 to his ex-wife's house. She had called him a few minutes ago, a blabbering mess, unable to keep control of her emotions long enough to make any sense over the phone. All he knew was that it had something to do with their son, Josh. So he left in the middle of a meeting with his team and jumped on the road. On the way, he called Josh's phone but didn't get an answer. This was nothing new. His son rarely took his calls.

Zegers let out a frustrated sigh. He really didn't have time to deal with this kind of crap from his ex-wife right now. He'd gotten nowhere today in his search for Parker Barnes. His team had been in and out of nearly every crack and crevice of the city, and the boy was still nowhere to be found. Several street kids said they recognized his photo but hadn't seen him around lately. Zegers was now considering posting bulletins about Parker on street corners and promising a financial reward for any info that led to locating him. He knew the move was desperate and would likely bring out a host of crazy calls, but he had to somehow find that damn kid.

Zegers traversed the quaint neighborhood of nearly matching brick homes before finally skidding to a stop at the curb outside his house—or his *former* house. He jumped from the Jeep and hurried up to the front door. Lisa answered immediately. She was still sobbing, with tears streaming down her face.

"What the hell, Lisa? Talk to me already."

"I'm sorry. It's Josh—"

"I know it's Josh. I got that much on the phone before you cracked up on me. Is he hurt? Is he okay?"

Zegers looked past her into the house but spotted no sign of his son.

"I don't know," Lisa stammered. "Because I can't find him."

More sobs. Zegers wanted to scream at his ex-wife for further information but knew that wouldn't do any good. Lisa never was able to control herself. So instead, he put two hands on her shoulders, gently squeezed, and looked her in the eyes.

"Hey, it's okay," he reassured her. "I'm here. Just calm down. Let's go inside, and you can tell me what happened."

She nodded. They moved inside the house and sat down at a small round table in the front room. The room used to be Zegers's home office, but Lisa had turned it into some kind of artsy room. There was an easel in the corner with a half-painted canvas on it. Looked like a vase with flowers. The table was covered in all kinds of craft materials. It always felt like a kick in the gut to come back inside his own house and see it completely changed. Which was why he usually just waited in the car for Josh to come out. Of course, that hadn't been happening too much lately—thanks to Lisa and the judge. But he didn't have time for those emotions right now.

Lisa caught her breath. "Josh didn't come home from football practice today. He was supposed to catch a ride with Andrew's dad. But Andrew said he watched Josh get into someone else's car. When he didn't show up, I started calling his phone, but he didn't answer."

"Okay, so what? Maybe he's goofing off with some other friends. Boys will be boys, Lisa. Even when you try to make him into a girl."

She shot him daggers, and he regretted saying it.

"I'm sorry," he said.

"It's more than that, Harry. I wouldn't be freaking out because he ditched his ride and won't answer my phone calls."

"Then why're you freaking out?"

"He sent me this text twenty minutes ago."

She pulled out her phone and showed it to Zegers. A simple five-word text from Josh: The food here is great.

He looked back at Lisa with a furrowed brow.

"What the hell does that mean?" he asked.

"It's a code we had when he was in middle school. He was supposed to text me this phrase if he felt like he was ever in trouble somewhere. Maybe if someone was doing drugs, or he felt like he was in a bad spot somehow. He would send me this, and I would come and get him so he wouldn't look bad with any of his friends. I'd just look like the over-protective mom."

"That's smart. Did he ever use it?"

She shook her head. "Not once. Until today."

That left a sinking feeling in Zegers's stomach. "Andrew didn't recognize who picked Josh up?"

"Andrew didn't know. He said it was a yellow Camaro with black racing stripes. A *cool car*, he said. But he'd never seen it before today."

"But Josh willingly got into the car?"

"I guess. Andrew didn't act like it was a big deal."

"It's probably not. Did you use Find My Phone?"

"I tried. His phone is turned off."

Zegers considered what Lisa had said. Josh never turned his phone off. His son treated the device like it was his oxygen supply. Why would he do it now? Could someone have forced him to do it? And why did Josh feel like he was in some kind of trouble? Zegers shook his head, again frustrated at having to deal with this right now. It was probably not a big deal. Teenage boys do dumb things. Hell, Zegers had done more than his fair share in high school. Josh had probably just fallen in with a bad crowd. This could be nothing more than him sitting around in someone's bedroom where other boys were smoking weed. A big part of Zegers wanted to start yelling at his ex-wife, berating her for allowing Josh too many freedoms. This is why she should've never forced the custody issue. Josh needed his father around. But at the same time, he knew she had plenty of ammunition to yell right back at him. If Josh had gotten involved in something bad, it was equally his fault. He'd driven his whole family away. Now was not the time to point fingers.

"I didn't know what else to do but call you," Lisa explained.

"No, you did the right thing. I'm sorry I yelled at you."

"You have to find him, Harry. I'm so worried."

"Hey, I'll find him. I promise. Josh will be okay. I'll make sure of it."

TWENTY-SIX

David sat across a café booth from Jess. He ate a cheeseburger while Jess munched on a BLT. A few papers were spread out on the table between them. Jess had taken Maylor's latest phone bill from his trailer. They were searching phone numbers online, trying to see if any were registered to someone with the name Dilly. So far, no luck. Unfortunately, the last phone call registered on the phone bill was from ten days ago. So they had no clue about Maylor's latest calls. They'd already searched Google for any mention of the name Dilly with some kind of connection to Maylor or their current situation, but found nothing. They were getting nowhere fast. And typing in *Dilly* + *Austin* only brought up a list of hundreds of random names and businesses. All of which led them down pointless rabbit holes.

"You think Parker's okay?" Jess asked, nibbling on a fry.

David sighed, glanced out a front window. "He's a tough kid."

"And resourceful. You really seem to be fond of him."

"I think I see a lot of myself in him. We both lost our parents young, so I understand a lot of the pain and anger he's carrying around. Parker needs someone consistent in his life who can encourage him in a positive way. Someone he can learn to trust. I hoped to offer him that—but now everything has blown up on us."

"You're doing everything you can, David."

"I know. But if something happens to him—and by *something*, I think you know what I mean—it will haunt me my whole life. I probably should have made him talk to the FBI yesterday instead of shielding him. I thought I was protecting him, but I only made matters worse."

"You made the decision you felt was best in the moment. You didn't know everything."

"I guess. But I can't lie and say my pride didn't influence it. Zegers was challenging me, and it felt good to stand up to him."

"Well, Zegers has that effect on people. He didn't bring out the best in me, either."

They shared a slight smile.

"Still nothing on your end?" David asked, nodding at the phone numbers.

She shook her head. "Not yet."

"I'm going to call the boys, see if they have any updates for us."

David stood, walked out in front of the café, and began checking in with his crew. Larue was hitting all the hot spots around campus. He mentioned that a couple of street kids told him "FBI dudes" were out there showing everyone a photo of Parker. He'd managed to track down Skater, whose cell phone had been turned off since yesterday because he couldn't make the payment. Skater claimed he hadn't seen or heard from the boy since the night Parker was arrested. But he wanted to help them with the search. Curly and Shifty had had no luck so far, either. They were walking a fifteen-block radius around the Hand-Up Home in case Parker hadn't traveled a great distance from the facility before hunkering down somewhere. Doc was checking hospitals, just in case an unidentified boy matching Parker's description showed up at one of them. But he hadn't.

David turned when he heard a sudden knock on the restaurant window. Jess was enthusiastically waving him back inside. He said goodbye to Doc, hung up, and hurried back inside the café.

"Tell me," David said, sliding into their booth.

She slid the phone list in front of him. She'd circled one of the numbers. "This phone number belongs to someone named Dillon Dyson. So I looked him up. Get this: Dyson owns the Burping Goat."

"Then that's got to be our Dilly, right?"

Jess showed him her phone screen, where she'd pulled up an article from a local music magazine. There was a photo of a fiftysomething man in a gray suit with his arm around country star Willie Nelson. The caption below the photo said, "Dilly Dyson hosts Willie Nelson Night at Dance Texas." David examined the man. Fit and tan, Dyson looked kind of like a young Jeff Bridges.

"This was from a couple of years ago," Jess explained. "Since then, Dyson filed for bankruptcy and had to close down his bar Dance Texas, along with several others. I think the Burping Goat might be the only bar he still has open."

"Great work, Jess."

"Thanks. According to the phone bill, Maylor called and received calls from this number several times leading up to the end of this statement's billing cycle."

"So the two men have some kind of established relationship."

"It would appear so. But I can't find a connection between Dyson and Kingston. I just ran an online search, and nothing popped up tying the two men together in any way."

David considered that. "I guess this could be nothing. Hard to know for sure if what the girlfriend said was truly legitimate."

"What if I call the number? Just see if he answers?"

"And if he does?"

"I'll ask him about Maylor and see what kind of response we get."

"Okay, go for it."

Jess typed in the number, put her phone on speaker, and set it between them. It rang four times and then went to an automated voice mail. She hung up. "I'd rather we have a live conversation with him to better gauge his response."

"The Burping Goat is not far from here, right?"

"Right. Let's go see if he's there."

As they began collecting papers from the table, David's phone buzzed. A random number. He hated picking up calls from people he didn't know. He wasted a lot of hours on the phone giving legal advice to strangers who'd gotten his number from one of his homeless friends. But he couldn't take the chance of ignoring any calls today.

"This is David," he answered, rubbing his forehead.

A long pause, then, "I'm scared, Mr. Adams."

David stiffened, felt adrenaline course through him.

"Where are you, Parker?"

Jess looked over at him with wide eyes. David nodded.

"Hiding."

"Are you okay? Are you hurt?"

"I'm okay. Just . . . scared. I don't know what to do."

David glanced out the café window. The gray Buick was parked in the lot. For a second, David wondered if the FBI would've tapped his phone. It was the first time he'd even thought about it. Could they be listening in on this conversation? He doubted it. Surely there was no way a judge would have granted a phone tap at this point.

"I'm scared, too, Parker. I'm not okay with you being out there on the streets. It's not safe."

"I have no choice, Mr. Adams. People are after me."

"I know."

"You do?"

"The FBI is not very happy with me right now."

"Not just the FBI. Other bad people."

David wondered what Parker knew about Richie Maylor. "What other bad people, Parker?"

"That's the thing, Mr. Adams. I don't know. I need your help."

David was glad to hear him say that. "How are you calling me?"

"I'm in a grocery store. I borrowed a phone from a lady. I told her I needed to call my parents. She's standing about ten feet away from me but can't hear what I'm saying. But I need to be quick."

It was the same smart maneuver the boy had used last night to get a phone and leave him the voice mail. As Jess had mentioned, he was resourceful. Not too many people were going to turn away an innocent-looking boy like Parker who wanted to call his parents. David was beginning to formulate a plan.

"Are you anywhere near downtown?" David asked.

Parker didn't respond.

David pressed him. "You have to trust me right now, Parker."

"I want to. I really do. But I'm scared to trust anyone."

"Do you know where the Paramount Theatre is on Congress Avenue in the middle of downtown? It has the big vertical sign outside that says *Paramount*."

"Is that the place that has the shows and movies?"

"Yes, that place."

"Yes, sir, I know it."

"Can you easily get there?"

"I can walk there. It'll probably take me twenty minutes or so."

David checked his watch. "Okay, I want you to meet me in the alley behind the Paramount Theatre in twenty minutes. Will you do that?"

More silence, then, "Yes, sir. I'll be there."

Parker hung up. David felt his heart racing.

"Twenty minutes?" Jess asked him.

David nodded. "Hopefully enough time for me to ditch my annoying shadow."

"How're going to do that?"

"I'm not sure yet."

"Can I help?"

"Yes, by going to the bar. See if you can find this Dyson guy."

"Okay. Keep me posted about Parker."

As Jess moved past him toward the café's front door, David grabbed her by the hand. She turned to look at him.

"Be safe, okay, Jess?"

"I think you know by now I can take care of myself."

"I do. But I have a bad feeling about this."

She squeezed his hand. "I will."

TWENTY-SEVEN

David felt his adrenaline suddenly racing. He was at once relieved to hear Parker was okay but now fully stressed about how to get to the boy without bringing the FBI along with him. He quickly drove back to his office and parked in a nearby paid lot. As he headed for the front of his building, he watched the gray Buick ease to the curb of Congress Avenue. David bounded up the stairs to the second level. Once inside his personal office, David reached into his desk drawer, found a second cell phone that he'd been allowing Doc to use here and there for law firm business. He turned it on to make sure it was fully charged, then turned it back off to preserve the battery. He then circled around his desk, hit the stairs again, and left the building. The sidewalks were busy with people shopping and heading out early to bars and restaurants. From the corner of his eye, he caught the two federal agents pop out of the Buick behind him.

Darting in and out of people, David kept a brisk pace. But not so fast as to lose the two agents—yet. He wanted to lead them as far away as possible before hopefully ditching them. Walking north up Congress Avenue, David made his first pass outside the Paramount Theatre. The place was one of those classic old-school theaters that had been around since the early 1900s. If there was a feature film coming out with some kind of connection to Austin—either by being filmed around the city or through a famous local actor—it usually premiered at the Paramount. David had mentioned it to Parker because he thought the kid might know its exact location.

David continued to head north, pausing at streetlights as cars passed, taking brief moments to make sure the two agents were still back there somewhere. He cut across to the other side of Congress Avenue two blocks from the Texas Capitol building. Jeter and Hernandez stayed right behind him. At that point, David pulled out his phone, brought up the Uber app, and—while continuing to walk—requested a ride. He chose a pickup location two blocks away and tried to time it just right. He paused at a streetlight while watching a block ahead of him for the white Jeep Cherokee that his Uber app said was about to arrive. When he spotted the vehicle, David hustled forward. He was running now. He didn't care if the two agents figured out what he was doing. It was go time.

Getting to the Jeep Cherokee, he jumped in the back and immediately told the driver, "Please go, now. I'm in a hurry!"

"Sure, pal."

The driver—a midforties man named Dennis with a crew cut—quickly pulled away from the curb into traffic. David turned around and spotted the two FBI agents trying to run toward the car. David knew if Dennis didn't make it all the way through the next stoplight, Jeter and Hernandez might catch up. If they did, David had no idea what would happen next. Would they pull the car over on foot?

"Come on, Dennis. I need you to get me there."

"I'm on it. You're only going five blocks. Did you really need a lift?"

"Yes. Just go!"

Dennis maneuvered into a crowded right lane, cut someone off, and then swiftly sped up. The car easily made it through the stoplight. Then Dennis turned right on the next street. Watching through the back window, David could no longer see the two agents in pursuit.

They had gotten lost behind a set of buildings. But David knew they were probably already calling in the license plate of the Jeep Cherokee. He needed to get out right away. Within a few seconds, Dennis pulled his car over to the curb. David hopped out without a word, jumped up onto another crowded downtown sidewalk, and then cut into the first alley in sight.

Unless the FBI had a tracking device on his body somewhere, David was sure he had lost them. He checked his watch. He had five minutes to get back to Congress Avenue, where he prayed he would find Parker waiting for him. Arriving, he found the alley behind the Paramount surrounded on both sides by tall buildings. There were dumpsters and shadows but little else. It was a good place for a secret meeting. But where was Parker? David hoped the boy hadn't changed his mind. He heard a noise come from his left, but it was just a guy tossing trash into a dumpster from the back door of a business down the alley. The guy went back inside and closed the door.

David checked his watch again: 5:27. Come on, kid. Don't do this to me. More pacing in a nervous circle. If the kid didn't show, David didn't know what to do next.

At 5:28, David heard a voice behind him.

"Mr. Adams?"

He spun around, found Parker standing there wearing his black sweatshirt hoodie with the hood up over his head. The kid had some-how slipped into the alley without David ever hearing him. Parker looked uneasy. Like it took all the trust he could muster just to get to the alley, but he wasn't sure if he could take another step. David didn't make him. He hustled right over to the kid, knelt down, and hugged him tightly. Parker nearly collapsed into his strong arms, as if the weight of the whole world was falling off the boy's shoulders. David felt tears forming in his eyes. He didn't realize how much tension he'd been car-rying around for the past fourteen hours—ever since he'd gotten the call from Keith that Parker had run away.

"I'm happy to see you," David said.

David pulled back to examine the boy, make sure he really wasn't hurt. That's when he noticed that all Parker's hair was gone. The kid was fully bald. "What happened to your hair?"

"I cut it off. So they couldn't find me."

David nodded. Again, resourceful. He would ask later how the boy went about doing that. He didn't want to waste time on things that didn't matter at this point. They were still vulnerable to the FBI finding them.

"Will you come with me, Parker? I need to get you to a safe place so we can talk about what's happened."

"Is anywhere really safe, Mr. Adams?"

David swallowed. Fear was pouring out of every part of the boy right now. He needed to be reassured that it was possible to be safe. That someone would take care of him and protect him.

"Yes," David replied. "I know the perfect spot."

TWENTY-EIGHT

Because the FBI might try to track his next Uber ride, David grabbed a taxi so he could pay cash and get them out of downtown proper as fast as possible. Parker sat low in the back seat next to him. David had instructed him not to say anything during the ride. They didn't need their taxi driver overhearing something that might put them in some kind of jeopardy. Ten minutes into the drive, the driver pulled over into the parking lot of a Rudy's Country Store and Bar-B-Q and dropped them off. But they were not there to eat. The combo restaurant–gas station sat alone on its own property and backed up to the woods. Quickly guiding Parker around to the side of the building, David headed straight for the trees.

"Where are we going?" Parker asked, clearly confused.

"The safest place I know in this city. Trust me."

David took one more peek behind them, making sure no one was watching them. They were in the clear, so he turned and found a narrow strip of a trail that he knew well by now. They marched forward into the woods, cutting in and around tall trees and up and down small hills. There were no signs of this being a well-known path that people used regularly. David knew that it had been created by only one man. A good friend who liked to camp in complete isolation. A person he trusted probably more than anyone right now to protect Parker with his life.

About a quarter mile into their hike, just as the sun was setting and the skies were growing dark, David found the small clearing with the solo camping tent sitting next to a campfire. A small brown dog with a white spot that looked like a star on its back barked once, seemed to recognize David, then came bouncing over to him with great enthusiasm. David scooped the Yorkshire terrier right up.

"Hey, Sandy," he said, as the dog tried to lick him all over.

Then came a grouchy voice from inside the tent. "What the hell?"

A second later, a man in his late thirties stepped out. He had a full head of reddish-brown hair that flowed down past his shoulders and one of the thickest mustaches David had ever seen. Lean and muscular, the man wore a blue pearl-snap long-sleeve shirt, mostly unbuttoned, with blue jeans and cowboy boots.

"Hey, Rebel," David said. "How're you doing?"

The angry look on the man's face instantly vanished upon seeing David. It was quickly replaced with a grin that stretched from ear to ear. "Well, I'll be! If it ain't the Lawyer."

David handed the dog to Parker, who gladly started holding and petting Sandy. Then David and Rebel gave each other a hug. David had represented the homeless man six months ago on a big case. They had been good friends ever since. David tried to visit him here and there. He was probably the only person who even knew how to find Rebel.

"You doing okay?" David said.

"You know me, Lawyer. I'm causing trouble everywhere I can."

They both laughed.

"I'd expect nothing less," David said.

Rebel glanced over at Parker. "Who's the kid?"

"I want you to meet my friend Parker. We need a safe place right now."

Rebel glanced at David with narrowed eyes. "Yeah?"

"I need your help," David said, taking a more serious tone. "He's in danger."

"Well, all right. You came to the right place. Why don't I get this campfire going a bit more so we can all stay warm?"

Rebel shook Parker's hand, told a funny story about Sandy, and then invited them to sit around the campfire while he gathered some more wood to get it going again.

"You okay?" David asked Parker.

Parker nodded. The dog was sitting in his lap, enjoying every moment of the petting and attention the boy was giving him.

"I guess you like dogs?" David said.

"I love dogs. We had a golden retriever named Jordan. They took him away after my dad died and they hauled me off. I don't know what happened to Jordan."

"I'm real sorry. About everything that's happened to you."

Sandy kept crawling up Parker's chest and trying to lick his face. The boy didn't seem to mind. It was nice to see the kid grin.

"Your friend is funny," Parker mentioned. "Is his name really Rebel?"

"No, it's a nickname. He likes to call me *Lawyer*."

Another small grin. "I'm going to start calling you *Lawyer*, too."

David matched his grin. But it was time to get serious. "Parker, we need to talk about what all has happened, okay?"

Parker's grin disappeared. "I know."

"I need you to be truthful with me. It's the only way I can protect you."

Another nod. "I'm sorry for lying to you, Mr. Adams. I was there in the park the night that guy was killed. I was scared. And I just wanted to be left alone. But I guess that can't happen."

"No—not yet, at least. So what happened that night?"

Parker put Sandy down on the ground. The dog immediately raced off to go find Rebel in the woods around the campsite.

"I was sleeping in the park. On one of the picnic tables. A few of the guys I knew had been over there throwing a Frisbee around. They wanted to walk back over to campus when it started getting dark. But I was too tired. So I just decided to stay there and lie down on a picnic table. I was dead asleep when I heard this truck pull up to the park. The headlights woke me up. I jumped off the picnic table because I didn't want anyone to see me. And I kind of scooted off to the side behind some trees.

"A guy got out and just kind of hung out near the front bumper while smoking a cigarette. I wasn't sure what he was doing. I thought maybe he just drove over to the park to smoke or something. But a few minutes later, another car arrived. One of those fancy Cadillac Escalades. An older man got out and walked up to the other guy. And then it happened . . ."

Parker paused, noticeably swallowed.

"It's okay, Parker. Take a moment."

"It was scary, Mr. Adams. The guy smoking the cigarette suddenly pulled out a gun and aimed it at the other guy. They said a couple of things to each other, but I couldn't hear much. And then the younger guy shot the older guy in the chest. I think he did it twice, but it was real fast and loud. Not loud like a bang. It looked like the guy had one of those silencer things attached to his gun, like I see in movies sometimes. But the sound still vibrated in my chest. The older man staggered and fell down on his back. Then the guy with the cigarette stood over him and shot the man in the head. I couldn't believe it. I felt like I was having a nightmare or something. But it was real. I just sat there behind that tree, like, frozen or something."

David scooted closer to Parker, put his hand up on his shoulder, trying to comfort him. "What happened next?"

"After that, the guy in the truck split. He just pulled away and left the guy there in the grass. I couldn't take my eyes off him. I wasn't sure what to do. Then I saw the guy kind of twitch. He just kind of jerked a little bit. I thought he might still be alive. So I rushed over there to see for myself. It was the freakiest thing. The guy's eyes were still open, even though blood was pouring all down his face. I leaned down over him, started trying to talk to him. I thought if he was somehow still alive, maybe I could run off and get some help somewhere. I tried to lean in close to his chest to see if it was moving, but it wasn't. Then he was really still. He was dead."

"That must've been how you got the blood spot on the front of your shirt."

Parker pitched his head. "How do you know about that?"

"The FBI found your backpack with that shirt still inside. That's how they knew for sure you were there that night."

Parker's eyes widened. That seemed to spook him.

"What happened next, Parker?"

David needed to hear every detail.

"The guy in the truck suddenly came back. The headlights blinded me. But I could see it was the same truck as before. So I ran to the picnic table, grabbed my backpack, and took off running. I heard the guy jump out and start yelling at me. But I never slowed down. When I got to the woods, I took a quick look back. He was chasing after me. I just kept running as fast as I could, looking to get away from him. And then he tried to shoot me. I heard the same sound as before, and then I fell. Later, I saw that the bullet hit my backpack. It didn't get me. I got up and kept on running."

"Through the gas station parking lot?"

Parker looked up again. "Yes."

"That's where the FBI got the video of you. They saw you come out of the woods and run through the parking lot."

"Do they have a video of the guy chasing me?"

David shook his head. "No, he must've stopped."

"I was so scared, Mr. Adams. I thought about going to the police. But I didn't. I was afraid they would send me back to the Reid place when they found out I was a runaway. And I never wanted to go back there again."

"It's okay. I understand."

"After that, I just went back to my life on the streets and hoped it would all go away. Tried to forget it ever happened, just like I've tried to forget a lot of things the past couple of years. Maybe it would have worked if I hadn't gotten myself in trouble by stealing."

"Parker, was the guy at the park the same one you saw by the fence outside the courtyard at the Hand-Up Home yesterday?"

The boy's eyes went wide again. "How did you—"

"We saw it on a security camera. It looked like the guy threatened you."

"He did. It was the same guy. He showed me his gun and told me I should keep my mouth shut or else. That's why I ran, Mr. Adams. I knew I couldn't stay there with that guy knowing I was inside. I'd seen him kill a man already. I knew he would try to kill me, too. So I ran."

David pulled out his cell phone, showed Parker a mug shot of Richie Maylor from when he had been charged with felony assault years ago. "This is the guy?"

Parker nodded. "That's him. I saw him just a couple of hours ago, too."

David was shocked. "What? Where?"

"I was hiding out in an empty office building with some other guys. I thought it would be a safe place for a while, but it wasn't. The FBI showed up looking for me. They were showing my photo to everyone and asking if anyone had seen me. I barely got out of there without getting caught. But then a couple of blocks away, this guy with the goatee shows up out of nowhere with another guy, and they start chasing me. After I got away from them, I decided to call you. I knew I needed help."

David thought about what Parker had said. Richie Maylor showed up right after the FBI had been looking for Parker? Maylor had also shown up yesterday at the Hand-Up Home right after the FBI. Coincidence? Or was there something more to it?

"You did the right thing," he told Parker. "I'm going to help you."

"How? What do we do now?"

"I don't know yet. I need to figure that out."

Sandy came trotting back up to Parker, looking for some more petting. The kid scooped the dog right back up. Rebel piled a bunch of wood scraps onto the campfire and used a lighter to get the fire roaring again.

"You boys hungry?" Rebel asked. "I've got some canned chili I could get to cooking over the fire. How does that sound?"

David looked over to Parker, who quickly nodded.

"Sounds great, Rebel," David said.

Standing, David walked over closer to Rebel while he pulled the cans out of a backpack from inside the small tent. "I need to leave the boy here with you for a little while. You okay with that?"

Rebel shrugged. "Sure. I don't think Sandy has gotten this much loving in a long time. He can have the tent tonight. I'll sleep under the stars."

"I should be back later tonight. But, listen, you've got to protect this kid."

Rebel looked up with narrowed eyes. "What's going on, Lawyer?"

"Some bad people want him dead."

"Damn." Rebel glanced over at Parker. "Sweet kid. Don't seem right."

"It's not right. I need to go try to make it right."

"Don't you worry. I'll take good care of him."

David went back over to where Parker was playing with Sandy and knelt in front of him. "I have to leave you here with Rebel for a couple of hours."

Parker's face bunched up. "Why?"

"I have to try to go get your life back." He reached into his jacket pocket, pulled out the second phone he'd snagged from his desk drawer, and handed it to Parker. "In case of emergency."

"What are you going to do?"

"I don't know yet. But you're safe here, okay? Rebel won't let anyone hurt you. Believe me, you're safer with him than you are with me."

"You have to promise me you're coming back, Mr. Adams."

"I promise."

TWENTY-NINE

Jess had been sitting in a coffee shop for a half hour working on her phone when she finally got the text she'd been waiting for. After leaving the café earlier, she'd returned to the Burping Goat in search of Dilly Dyson. The cowboy bartender said his boss was not around but usually showed up at some point every night. They flirted for a little while, and Jess got the bartender to agree to text her whenever Dyson finally arrived. Cody seemed happy she'd been willing to hand over her phone number. Not that Jess had any real interest there—but perhaps somewhere else.

For a brief moment, she let her mind linger on David, and a small smile touched her lips. There was something about him that she really liked. A kindness and gentleness that reminded her a lot of her husband. Jeff would always bend over backward to help someone less fortunate. It was the kind of compassion that might have gotten him killed that tragic day out on the sidewalks of DC. Jess knew she'd let herself get hard over the past few years. It was fear-driven self-preservation. She did not ever want to feel that kind of pain again. But David was not hard—which surprised her. She'd done more investigating on him out of curiosity. She knew about him losing both parents at an early age.

Then she'd found out about the dangerous conspiracy he'd survived over at Hunter & Kellerman. Living through all that was enough to make anyone seriously cynical. But David was the opposite of that. Which she found attractive.

She glanced down at her phone and read the text from Cody again.

Boss man is here. Hope to see you soon.

She texted him right back: **On my way.** ☺

She left the coffee shop and headed for her car. Night was setting in as the last remnant of sun hit the horizon. The coffee shop was only a mile up the road from the bar, so it was a quick trip. She pulled into what was now a crowded parking lot in front of the Burping Goat. Trucks outnumbered cars three to one. She pushed through the front doors and found the place already rowdy. Country music blared from speakers, and the pool tables were surrounded. Most of the girls in the place wore painted-on jeans and cowboy boots, so Jess stood out a little in her black leather jacket, slacks, and heels. But that didn't stop several men from eyeballing her every move and flashing their best smiles as she made her way over to the bar. Cody spotted her right away and came over.

"Hey, beautiful," he said. "You want a drink?"

"Maybe in a second. Where is Mr. Dyson?"

Cody pointed over to a short hallway at the end of the bar. "First office on the right."

"You're a true sweetheart. Thanks."

"You bet. Come back for that drink."

Jess maneuvered through the crowd and made her way to the hallway. A thick guy with a buzz cut standing near the hallway entrance gave her a cocky smile as she passed. The bar did not lack for confident men. She poked her head inside the office and found

Dilly Dyson sitting behind a big wooden desk. He had on a tan suit with a white dress shirt and no tie, just like he'd been wearing in several of the photos she'd found of him online. That seemed to be his look. On the office wall behind him was a large painting of the Austin skyline. There were also several framed photographs of Dyson standing with popular country music stars. Dyson was staring at a laptop on his desk but looked up when he spotted her standing in the doorway.

"Mr. Dyson?" Jess said.

"Yes?"

"Do you have a minute?"

He looked her up and down, smiled. "Certainly."

Jess stepped fully into the office. Dyson got up out of his chair, circled around his desk, stuck out his hand. "You know my name, but I don't know yours."

She shook his hand. "Jess Raven."

"Good to meet you, Ms. Raven." He shut the door to his office behind them. "It gets so loud out there, I can hardly hear myself think sometimes."

"But loud means business is good, right?"

He smiled. "That's mostly true, I guess. What can I do for you?"

She decided to just come right out with it. "I'm looking for Richie Maylor. I heard he does some work for you."

Dyson cocked his head. "Heard from whom?"

"A girlfriend. Is it not true?"

"Why are you looking for Richie?"

Jess noted that he'd sidestepped her question. Which put her at a bit of a crossroads. At this point, she had no idea if any of this had anything to do with Dilly Dyson. Her only connecting point came from the jealous girlfriend. That certainly wasn't something to build a case on. Still, there was something about the way Dyson had so promptly shifted the conversation that gave her pause about being truthful with him. She had prepared to go down two different paths depending on her gut instinct in the moment.

She chose path B. "I work for an attorney representing the estate of someone who has left Mr. Maylor some money. But I'm having trouble locating him. I hoped you could help with that."

"Really? How much money?"

"Well, I can't say, Mr. Dyson. That's private information."

"Please, call me Dilly."

"Okay. Do you know how I can find Mr. Maylor?"

"Possibly. What attorney did you say you worked for?"

"I didn't."

Jess smiled, left it at that. If Dyson wasn't going to answer her questions, she didn't feel obligated to respond to his. But the deeper this conversation went, the more suspicious she became of the man. Why so much shadowboxing? Was he just that kind of guy? Or could he possibly be involved with the death of the federal witness? She couldn't be sure at this point. But she wanted to be more careful now that she'd met the guy.

Dyson shrugged. "Well, I'm not sure where Richie is at the moment. Honestly, I barely know the guy. He's done some odd jobs around the bar for me, but that's about it. Nothing more than that. But if you leave me your number, I'll try to see if I can track him down for you. Would that help?"

"Yes, I'd really appreciate it."

Dyson grabbed a notepad off his desk and handed her a pen. Jess quickly scribbled down a fake phone number.

"Can I buy you a drink?" Dyson offered.

"No, I'm fine. But thank you. I really have to get going."

"Okay. You have a good night, Ms. Raven."

Jess slipped out of the office. She considered hanging around the bar, seeing if she could dig up any more relevant information on Dyson, until she got an urgent text message from David.

Meet me back at the office ASAP. I have Parker.

Jess rushed for the front doors.

THIRTY

Jess called David while driving down the MoPac Expressway on her way back downtown. Traffic was still thick out on the highway.

"Where are you?" David asked.

"In my car on my way to you. You have Parker?"

"Yes. I was able to get him off the streets. He's with a friend until I can figure out what to do next."

"You left Parker with a friend?"

"Trust me—this is no ordinary friend."

"You and your odd friends."

"The kid saw it all, Jess. Richie Maylor shot Max Legley in the park that night. Parker was there and nearly got himself killed. Then Maylor showed up today and nearly got him again."

"Are you serious? How did he find Parker?"

"I have no idea. Did you find Dyson?"

Jess switched lanes to get out from behind a slow-moving van, punched the gas down again. "Yes, I spoke with him a few minutes ago. I can't tell yet if he has anything to do with this. He was cryptic in his answers about knowing Maylor. It made me suspicious, but that doesn't mean he's the reason Max Legley is dead. Especially when we can find no connection to Kingston."

"Yeah, I hear you. How far out are you?"

"Probably ten minutes."

"Get here as fast as you can. We need to make a plan on how we're going to help Parker get out of this mess."

Jess tossed her phone onto the passenger seat and pressed the gas pedal down even harder. She took the First Street exit and quickly drove into downtown proper. A minute later, she pulled into a parking spot right along the curb of Congress Avenue only a block away from David's office building. Jess leaned over to grab her workbag from the other seat and then got out.

Before she could take another step, she heard a car engine rumble loudly behind her. Then she spotted the bright headlights of a yellow Camaro coming right at her at rapid speed.

Jess froze. The car was not swerving. Whoever was driving wanted to hit her. Suddenly, a strong push on her shoulder came from the side. She toppled out of the way just as the car reached her. In a blur, she spotted the man who had shoved her take a direct hit from the vehicle, flip up onto the hood, hit the windshield, and then topple off onto the pavement about fifteen feet away from her.

Jess scrambled to her feet. The Camaro slowed for only a moment. Whoever was driving took a peek back at the scene, as if surveying the damage. Jess cursed. She recognized the face of the driver. It was the same thick guy with the buzz cut who had smiled at her in the hallway of the bar earlier. The guy turned, punched the gas. The tires squealed, and the car sped away.

Jess rushed over to the man who had just saved her life. Looking down, she couldn't believe it. It was Bobby E. Lee, the elderly man with the white beard in the Civil War uniform who sat outside David's office every day. Bobby Lee was moaning and bleeding all over his face and body. One of his legs was twisted completely backward and looked broken in several places. Finding her phone, Jess quickly called 911. She reported the hit-and-run and gave the operator her location.

A crowd quickly began to gather around them. Bobby Lee yelled out again in pain.

Jess dropped to her knees next to him, took his bloody right hand in hers, and held it to her chest. Leaning in close, she said, "Hang in there, Bobby. You're going to be okay. Help is on the way. Just hang in there with me a little longer."

Police cars and an ambulance arrived within minutes. The medics had to nearly pry Jess away from Bobby so they could get better access to him. She kept thanking the old man over and over again, tears now streaming down her cheeks. After quickly inspecting him, the medics strapped Bobby Lee onto a stretcher, hoisted him up into the back of the ambulance, and climbed inside with him.

David was suddenly standing next to her. "Jess? Are you okay? What happened?"

Jess turned to him. "Bobby Lee just saved my life."

David's head whipped back toward the ambulance that was now pulling away with sirens wailing and lights blaring.

"Bobby Lee is in that ambulance?"

"Yes. We have to go to the hospital with him right now."

He grabbed her hand. "I'll take you. Let's go."

THIRTY-ONE

David and Jess huddled in a small hospital waiting room down the hallway from where Bobby Lee was in emergency surgery. One of the doctors had told David earlier that the old man was in bad shape. A lot of broken bones and severe lacerations. The extent of the internal injuries was unknown. It would be touch and go for a while. The first couple of hours were crucial. The doctor was making no promises of anything at this point. Then he left them alone to sweat it out.

"I must've spooked him," Jess said to David.

"Who? Dyson?"

"Who else? This happened right after I spoke with him."

"Spooked him enough to where he would immediately send someone after you to try to take you out?"

"I'm telling you, David. I saw the driver of that yellow Camaro. He was the same guy from the bar. He must've followed me."

"You didn't notice the car behind you on the drive downtown?"

She shook her head. "But I was so focused on getting here as quickly as possible that I wasn't paying close attention."

David sighed, ran a hand through his hair. Everything with this case seemed to be spiraling into chaos. "Take me back through your whole conversation with Dyson again."

David had already heard it once but wanted to hear it a second time. Jess had still been rattled when first telling him about the encounter. She was calmer now. Maybe he missed something. She told him the story again.

His brow furrowed. "You didn't mention anything about leaving a fake phone number with him the first time around."

"You're right," she said, eyes widening. "Maybe Dyson called the number right after I walked out of there. And when he realized I'd lied about it, he decided to take action."

David cursed. "I'm calling Zegers. Try to work something out. If we're dealing with someone who was willing to run you down after one ambiguous conversation, there's no telling what they might do next."

"I agree. Parker needs to be brought in ASAP."

David headed for the hallway, then turned around when he realized Jess was not coming with him. "You're staying?"

"I'm not leaving here until I know Bobby is going to be okay."

He nodded. "Keep me posted."

"You do the same."

THIRTY-TWO

David met Zegers at the foot of Buford Tower, which sat four blocks from his office along the running trails of Lady Bird Lake. The old bell tower was a city landmark built in the 1930s. David often ran past it on his early-morning jogs. Night had fallen on the city, and the streets were beginning to clear of traffic. He thought about Parker sitting around the campfire with Rebel right now. He hoped the kid was doing okay. He knew Rebel had an endearing way of connecting with people and making them feel comfortable—even if some of his stories were right out of *The Twilight Zone*. Plus, having the dog around had sure seemed to brighten Parker's spirits. The kid ached for some childhood normalcy in the worst way possible. David hoped to be able to give him something like that very soon.

He watched as Zegers walked up to him wearing a gray sweatshirt and jeans, not his usual sport coat and slacks. The agent's eyes were red, and his hair was disheveled.

"You look like hell, Harry," David said.

"Well, it's been a helluva a day in more ways than one. What do you want, David? I'm really busy right now. Not only do I have this case, but my son decided today would be a good day to take off with the wrong kids after school and not tell his mom. And because my ex is an emotional mess, I'm the one who's been on the phone all evening with other parents, trying to find him. So unless you're going to tell me where I can find Parker Barnes, I'd have preferred to have had this conversation with you over the phone instead of driving way the hell down here like you insisted."

"I have Parker."

Zegers jerked slightly back, eyes flashing. "You do?"

"Yes, he reached out to me this afternoon. I picked him up. He's in a safe place right now."

"So that's why you pulled the stunt with my guys earlier?"

David shrugged. "Hope there are no hard feelings."

"Well, I can't say they didn't get a good ass chewing from me for letting some lawyer outwit them. So where is Parker?"

"Not so fast. I want a deal."

Zegers's eyes narrowed. "What kind of deal?"

"I want a witness protection package for him. I want him to have a brand-new life somewhere with special privileges. The kind of privileges that have been ripped away from him over the past few years."

"Well, hold on a second, David. I need to know what the kid knows first. I can't just go requesting—"

"Parker was there in the park that night, Harry. He saw the whole thing. Which nearly got him killed."

"He can ID the shooter?"

"Yes. Parker knows him by face. But I can give you his name."

"What? How?"

"We launched our own investigation to try to help Parker."

"Sounds like you should come work for me."

"Actually, I think I'm doing much better on my own, thank you."

Both of them remained quiet for a moment as two pedestrians passed by them. Zegers waited until they were clear to speak again.

"So you're telling me you can give me the name of the shooter, and Parker is willing to point him out of a lineup?"

"I still have to clear this with Parker. But, yes, and that's not all. I think we have a good lead on whom the shooter might be working for, too."

"Who is *we*?"

"Jess Raven is helping me."

He rolled his eyes. "Figures."

"Look, she's not my girlfriend, Harry, so relax. She was just messing with you this morning. She's doing pro bono work for my firm."

"So she told you what happened between us?"

"We all strike out sometimes, brother. Let it go."

Zegers sighed, crossed his arms. "Stop playing games here, David. If you're so smart, tell me who's behind this thing right now."

"I want the package first. Then we'll talk."

"How about I just throw your ass in jail?"

David shook his head. "Who's playing games now?"

Zegers huffed. "You're really annoying, you know that?"

"Thanks, I feel the same about you. How long do you think it will take you?"

"To get a witness protection package approved? Hell, it could take days."

"How about you call me in an hour with the good news?"

Zegers's eyes narrowed. "Listen, if I go to bat for this and use what little capital I have to push this kind of thing through, you'd better be telling the damn truth. Or, believe me, I will throw your ass in jail."

THIRTY-THREE

Jess paced the hallways of the hospital for an excruciatingly long time until the doctor finally came out to talk to her. She damn near held her breath while waiting for the first words to come out of his mouth. If he began with *we did everything we could*, she was going to break down in tears again. The thought of Bobby Lee having sacrificed his life to save hers after she'd been so awful to him—and her never having a chance to say how sorry she felt about the whole thing—might be too much for her to bear.

"He's going to make it," the doctor said.

Jess felt a flood of relief pour through her whole body.

"He's got a long road of recovery, mind you," the doctor continued. "But I think we've managed to put everything back together in a way that should help stabilize him. I gotta say, that's one tough old man."

"Can I see him?" Jess asked.

"He's out cold right now. Mr. Lee is pumped with so many meds, he'll probably sleep until tomorrow morning."

"I still want to see him. The guy saved my life."

He tilted his head. "I didn't realize that. Sure, come on."

Jess followed the doctor down a hallway through a couple of doors and into the ICU. Bobby Lee was in the first bed on her right.

A nurse was working around him, plugging different cords into various machines. The doctor told Jess to take as much time as she needed.

Jess stepped up to the bed and stared down at the old man. There were bandages on his face, but he otherwise looked peaceful. She still couldn't believe the man had put his own life at risk to save her out there on the street. She hadn't even noticed him on the sidewalk. But he must've noticed her. And in spite of her treatment of him, he made a move that she would never forget.

Leaning down, she gently kissed him on the forehead.

"I'm sorry, Bobby Lee. Thank you."

Ten minutes later, Jess was speeding north up the MoPac Expressway. She felt more determined than ever to find out if Dilly Dyson was behind the guy who'd tried to run her down. If they thought they could somehow scare her off, they were mistaken. They'd just messed with the wrong damn gal.

Pulling into the parking lot in front of the Burping Goat, she quickly scanned the cars to see if she could spot the yellow Camaro anywhere. It would be easy to find because the windshield had shattered when Bobby Lee had flipped up onto the hood. She didn't see it anywhere. Instead of parking in front of the bar, she pulled around to the back. There were several other vehicles parked there. Two BMWs, a Lincoln Navigator, an Audi SUV, a Mercedes sedan, and a shiny red Corvette. She wondered which might belong to Dyson. But first, she had to make sure Dyson was still inside the bar.

She pulled out her phone to text Cody, the bartender.

Hey, you still tending the bar?

She got a reply a few seconds later.
Cody: Yes ma'am. You coming back to me?

Jess: I'm here. Can you take a break and meet me out back?

Cody: Be there in two minutes!

Jess "hearted" his last message. Then she got out of her car and walked over to the back door of the bar. It was time to be aggressive in getting information. Cody stepped out within sixty seconds, looking pretty fired up at the prospect of seeing her again in private. Jess shut the door behind him and then kissed him full on the mouth until he staggered back against the dingy brick of the building. He tried to get handsy, but she pushed his arms down and stepped back for a moment.

"Wait, I need a favor first," she said.

"A favor? Sure, anything. What?"

"Is your boss still here?"

"Dilly? Yeah, he's here."

She turned to look over at the cars. "Which one of these belongs to him?"

Cody examined the lot. "The Mercedes. Why?"

"Just curious." She gave him another quick kiss, turned to walk back to her Explorer. "Thanks, Cody. I'll see you soon."

"Wait!" Cody called out. "You're leaving?"

"Can't stay. Gotta run."

"Aw, come on, Jess. Really?"

Jess smiled, got in her car, and pulled away.

She waited in the parking lot of a gas station only a block away from the bar for nearly an hour before she noticed the shiny black Mercedes sedan pull into the street in front of her. As the vehicle passed, Jess spotted Dyson sitting behind the steering wheel. She shifted into drive and then followed him.

Dyson drove at a casual pace for about fifteen minutes as he navigated the city until he pulled into a neighborhood of luxury homes. Jess wondered if this was where the man lived. Three blocks into the neighborhood, Dyson eased his Mercedes to the curb in front of a nice two-story white Colonial with a black Escalade parked under a porte cochere in a side driveway. Jess settled on the curb a half block back so she wouldn't be noticed. Climbing from his Mercedes, Dyson didn't walk straight up to the front door. Instead, he moved up the driveway to a side door. Jess eased her car forward slightly with the headlights off to get a better look. Dyson knocked. A few seconds later, an attractive blonde in probably her late thirties answered the door. She immediately looked familiar, but Jess couldn't place her. Dyson and the blonde began speaking about something while standing in the open doorway.

Pulling out her phone, Jess typed in the address for the house. When the results popped up, she cursed. According to public appraisal records, the Colonial belonged to Max and Christina Legley. Max Legley was the dead federal witness. Christina was the man's wife—or widow. The woman looked familiar to Jess because she'd seen several photos of her standing with her husband while doing research on the federal tax fraud case. But what the hell was Dyson doing at her house?

Jess suddenly got nervous. Could Dyson possibly be there to harm the woman? Was Christina Legley's life in danger right now? For a second, Jess considered pulling out her handgun and making a move toward the house. But then she paused. The conversation did not look hostile in any way. Nor did it look awkward. These two were not strangers. Christina Legley clearly knew this man, even though Jess had been unable to find any connection between Dyson and her husband.

Using her phone's camera, Jess zoomed in as close as she could and began snapping pictures of the two of them talking. Suddenly, the conversation took a turn in a direction Jess didn't anticipate. The two of them embraced and began passionately kissing. What the hell? Jess continued to take pictures on her phone. Within seconds, Christina had pulled Dyson all the way inside the house with her and shut the door behind them. Jess put her phone down, stunned.

Christina Legley's husband had been dead for only a week. The body was still warm. Which led Jess to believe the woman was having an affair with Dilly Dyson long before her husband ever saw a bullet in that park.

THIRTY-FOUR

David sat with Parker and Rebel around the campfire. Rebel continued to tell story after story about his life out on the streets, all the famous movie stars he'd met throughout the years, his various hijinks and escapades with the police in different cities, and so on and so forth. David knew half of the stories were pure fiction—Rebel had a unique way of drifting in and out of reality—but it didn't really matter because the man kept making Parker laugh. And it was great to see the carefree side of the boy. Parker seemed the most relaxed he'd been since David had first met him.

Rebel grabbed a bag of marshmallows out of his tent and began poking them on the ends of sticks so Parker could roast them over the campfire.

Even though it was great to see Parker in good spirits, David was a nervous wreck. He kept checking his phone every few seconds, waiting to get word back from Zegers. An hour had already come and gone with nothing to show for it. If the FBI agent was unable to pull off the witness protection package, David wasn't sure what to do next. He'd already played his hand by telling Zegers how much they knew. The FBI would still want that information. David would have to play legal hardball and be willing to go the court route in order to try to protect the boy. It would turn into a big mess. He was counting on Zegers. But maybe that was a mistake.

Rebel was doing some kind of campfire dance with his marshmallow stick, cracking Parker up, when David finally got a text from Zegers. He stared at his phone and then let out a sigh of relief.

Package approved. Let's get this show on the road!

David texted back: **Am I going to like it?**

Trust me. The kid is going to be living much better than you and me.

Although relieved, David was guarded. He had not yet shared anything about this possibility with Parker. He didn't want to mislead the boy if Zegers couldn't pull it off. But it was now time to have that discussion.

"Hey, Parker, we need to talk about something."

Parker turned to him while shoving a blackened, gooey marshmallow in his mouth. As if sensing something was up, Rebel said he was going to look for more firewood and called Sandy over to him.

"What is it?" Parker asked.

David measured his words. "What would you say if I could get you a new life somewhere else? Something so much better than what you've had the past couple of years? New clothes, new opportunities, a clean slate, where I could guarantee you'd be well taken care of."

Parker's eyes grew to slits. "A person doesn't get something like that for nothing, Mr. Adams."

"You're right. You'd have to tell the truth about everything."

"To the FBI?"

"Yes. And eventually in a courtroom."

"Would I still be in danger?"

"No, you would be protected by US Marshals in something called the Witness Protection Program."

"I've seen that in the movies a few times. It doesn't always go well."

"That's the movies, Parker. It's not like that."

"Where would I go?"

David shrugged. "You might get to choose."

"Anywhere I want?"

"Within certain parameters, but yes. We've been offered a package by the FBI to put you into the program. I would fully review it to sign off on it and make sure everything was right for you."

Parker picked at his sticky fingers. "All I'd have to do is tell the truth?"

"Yes, just tell the truth."

Parker turned more fully to him. "Would I still get to see you? If I was in this witness program?"

David had already been thinking about that. The thought of not personally being the one to help Parker move forward from here really stung. But he could think of no other way. Parker had to be protected. "No, you wouldn't. In order for you to be fully protected, you'd probably have to walk away from everything—including me."

More picking at his fingers. "You'd be okay with that, Mr. Adams?"

Hell no, David wanted to say. But he didn't.

"I just want you safe. I want you to get another chance at this life. You deserve that opportunity."

"I don't know. You really think we can trust the FBI?"

"Yes. And you can trust me."

"Okay. I trust you." A small smile crossed the boy's lips. "I've always wanted to go to Arizona and see the Grand Canyon. You think that's somewhere I could live in this program?"

David grinned. "I can for sure make that request."
David pulled his phone back out and texted Zegers.

Where?

Zegers texted right back. How about outside your office building?
David: Email me the proposal to review. If I like it, we'll be there in half an hour.

THIRTY-FIVE

Richie Maylor parked his truck on a downtown street four blocks away from his intended target. He found a spot where he could quickly pull out and be on I-35 seconds later. It would be critical for him to have a swift getaway. He checked the time on his phone, knowing every second counted right now. He needed to be ready. Reaching behind him to the back seat of the truck, he grabbed the long brown rifle bag he'd carried with him many times up to his cousin's deer lease. He was an expert with the hunting rifle. He'd once hit a white-tailed deer at nearly three hundred yards.

But he would not be shooting a clueless deer today.

Stepping out of the truck, he shifted the bag's strap over his shoulder and hit the sidewalk at a brisk pace. His heart was beating so fast right now. He really needed a joint to help calm him down. But he knew smoking weed might throw off his ability to perform the task at hand. And he couldn't let that happen. He passed several people out on the sidewalks and wondered if any of them were familiar with a hunting rifle bag. Would they find it odd that he was walking down the street with one?

It didn't really matter. He had to keep going.

He turned another street corner and rushed up the sidewalk. More checking the time on his phone, more nervous sweating. He was almost there. Arriving at the corner of Fifth and Congress Avenue, Richie glanced across the street and focused on a three-story redbrick building. He squinted in the glare of the streetlights. There didn't seem to be much activity outside the building at the moment.

Richie needed to hurry up and find a good hiding place to take the shot—while still being able to get himself out of the area as fast as possible. Right next to him was a three-story building that housed the Mexic-Arte Museum. If he could get to the roof, he'd have a perfect angle across the street. Turning around, Richie walked down to the sidewalk and then cut into the alley directly behind the building. He spotted a fire escape attached to the building that zigzagged up to the very top.

Taking a peek up and down the alley, he didn't see anyone that he thought mattered, so he grabbed the bottom rung of the metal ladder and hoisted himself up to the first landing. From there, he quickly climbed the stairs back and forth until he reached the top of the building. Swinging his legs over a short wall, Richie hustled across the flat roof and peered over the other side down onto Congress Avenue.

He smiled. Maybe fifty yards. No sweat.

It was the perfect spot to finally kill the boy.

THIRTY-SIX

David and Parker rode in the back of an Uber into downtown. Parker was understandably quiet. The boy's whole life was about to get flipped upside down again. David hoped this time it was for the good—although he knew having to deal with the FBI, federal prosecutors, lawyers, courtrooms, and all that jazz, would not be so good. David had tried to explain to Parker as much as possible what he thought would happen once they arrived and met with Zegers and his team.

But the truth was, David didn't really know.

The Uber driver drove down Fifth Street toward Congress Avenue. David's office building was only four blocks away now.

"You okay?" David whispered to Parker.

The boy looked over to him. "I'm really nervous."

"Me, too. But I'll be there for every step of it."

Parker nodded, stared back out the car window.

The Uber driver reached Congress, turned right. David immediately spotted Zegers and a small group of other FBI agents up ahead, huddled right outside the main doors of his office building. He could feel his gut twisting into knots. Parker was about to go through something no kid should ever have to endure—after having already had to bear so much. But there was no other way out of this.

The driver pulled the car over to the curb just up the street from Zegers. David got out first, and Parker followed. They stepped up onto the sidewalk together. Parker immediately reached over and grabbed David's hand. Zegers noticed them and began swiftly moving in their direction, along with five other agents. David noted that Farley, Jeter, and Hernandez were part of the group. Within seconds, they were quickly surrounded by the full weight of the FBI. To his credit, Zegers knelt in front of Parker and tried to offer the boy a warm welcome.

"Parker, my name is Agent Zegers. I know this must be overwhelming to you, but I promise I'm going to take very good care of you. You don't have to worry about anything. Okay?"

Parker nodded but squeezed David's hand even harder.

Zegers stood again, looked at David. "Thanks for coming."

"Like you said, let's get this show on the road."

"How about we go inside your office to go over everything?"

"Sounds like a plan."

The group of them began moving up the sidewalk together toward the front doors of the building. The first shot came with a loud bang and hit Agent Hernandez in the back of his right shoulder. Blood squirted across David's face. Hernandez let out a painful grunt and fell forward.

David heard the loud pop but at first thought maybe it was a car backfiring. Zegers spun around, his eyes flashing with panic. Agent Jeter immediately tackled Parker to the concrete and knocked David over to his right in the process. Another loud bang. The second shot hit Jeter square in the back. He flinched and grimaced in pain. Parker was directly beneath him. Had he also been shot?

David scrambled to get to Parker, who was pinned beneath the wounded agent. He could hear screams coming from bystanders on the sidewalks. He saw Zegers, Farley and the other two agents pull out their guns while scanning the area across the street and looking to fire back at the shooter. What the hell was happening?

A third loud bang rang out, and a chunk of the building exploded right next to David, sending shards of brick straight into his face. For a second, he couldn't see anything. But he could hear the FBI agents firing their guns. David blinked several times, trying to get the particles out of his eyes so he could find his way. When he could finally see again, David went for Parker. He had to get the boy out of there. But Parker was no longer underneath Jeter, who was still lying on the concrete.

Panicked, David whipped his head left and right. Where was Parker?

More shots fired around him. David ducked low. Who was trying to take them out? Had someone been staking out his office? Waiting for David to come back? Or was it something else? He again thought about what Parker had said earlier regarding Richie Maylor showing up right after the FBI had nearly grabbed him today. Could someone on Zegers's team have betrayed them?

David suddenly spotted the back of the boy sprinting up the sidewalk away from them. Then the boy took a sharp left and was gone.

"Parker!" David yelled as loud as he could.

THIRTY-SEVEN

David paced furiously around his office. His head was spinning, and his heart was pumping so fast, he thought it just might stop at any moment. Parker was gone. He couldn't believe it. The boy had managed to slip out in the middle of the chaos and had made a run for it. David had tried to chase after him but quickly got tripped up in the growing sidewalk crowds and the incoming swarm of police cars and emergency vehicles. David felt a panic inside him bigger than anything he'd ever experienced. He squeezed his hands together to try to stop his fingers from shaking.

Zegers was in his office with him, also pacing but on his phone barking at someone. David went to the front window again. Police cars, ambulances, and fire trucks covered the entire block in front of his office building. David had never seen so many uniformed officers. They scrambled to keep the crowd in its proper place and protect the scene. David stared across the street at the taller buildings on the other side. The shooter had been either inside or on top of one of those buildings. He couldn't be sure—it was all a nightmarish blur. Agents Hernandez and Jeter had both been hit. But fortunately, no one else—especially Parker.

David's eyes shifted from outside to his own reflection in the window. He still had blood splatter on his face. He took a sleeve and tried to wipe it off some more. But it just smeared. He needed to go wash his face in the restroom but didn't want to leave Zegers for even a moment in case any word came back on locating Parker. This was a nightmare.

Zegers finally hung up, cursed.

David turned. "Are they going to be okay?"

He knew Zegers had been talking with someone about Hernandez and Jeter, who were on their way to the hospital.

Zegers sighed. "I don't know. Hernandez might be okay. The bullet went through clean. They don't know about Jeter yet. They say it's bad."

"What the hell happened?" David asked Zegers for probably the fifth time in the past few minutes. "You promised me Parker would be safe."

Zegers just kept shaking his head. "I don't know."

"Could someone on your team have sold us out?"

Zegers shot him a glare. "Not a chance, David."

"How the hell else can you explain it, Harry? I didn't tell a single soul about our meeting. You were the only person I spoke with about it. But someone was clearly waiting for us to arrive out there."

Zegers considered that, cursed again, spun away from the window.

Farley came rushing into the office to join them.

"Anything?" Zegers questioned.

"Shooter was directly across the street on top of that art museum building. He left the rifle there. But we've been unable to locate him. We've got agents out searching everywhere. Police are trying to help. But it's an unbelievable mess out there."

"Get more agents down here," Zegers ordered. "Wake everyone the hell up. This is a damn emergency."

"I already have a call in for it."

"What about Parker?" David asked Farley.

Farley gave another sad shake of the head. "Sorry. No sign of him yet."

David put a hand on the back of his tight neck and squeezed. Where had the kid gone? Was he out there hiding close by? Or still running? Could he be making his way back to Rebel somehow? David would go there first upon leaving the office. And what was going through Parker's mind right now? The boy had been promised so much—and all of it had been ripped away from him in a hail of bullets.

The panic inside David continued to grow.

"Handle that rifle with care," Zegers instructed. "Maybe it'll lead us back to the shooter."

"Will do," Farley replied. "But it looks pretty clean. Any word on Hernandez or Jeter?"

"Hernandez is probably okay. Jeter is in really bad shape."

Farley hung his head. "You want me to call Jeter's wife?"

"No, I'll do it." Zegers gave a wary look at David, sighed, turned back to Farley. "Look, Farley, I want you to put our team under a microscope. The shooter may have been alerted from the inside to our situation with Parker. I want everyone who possibly knew about tonight scrutinized."

Farley frowned. "Come on, boss. No way."

"I want to be sure, Farley. So don't play favorites. And make our circle even tighter until we figure this out."

Farley nodded. "Okay, boss."

Zegers turned to David. "I don't want you talking to *anyone* other than me right now."

"I'll ask the same of you."

Zegers nodded. He gave Farley a few more instructions, and then the agent turned and headed out of the office. Zegers again joined David at the window. David kept staring at his cell phone, hoping he might receive an incoming call from Parker—but it was weak hope. There was no way the kid was going to make that call now. David had tried to call the cell phone he'd given Parker several times, but it always went straight to voice mail. The phone was off—which meant David also couldn't track the device with his Find My Phone app. If Parker turned on the phone, David would be able to know the boy's exact location. So he kept checking the tracking feature every few minutes. So far, nothing. David had to come to grips with the fact that he might never see or hear from Parker again.

"I promised the kid he'd be safe," David said, eyes on the scene below.

"So did I," Zegers mentioned. "We both failed him."

"He'll never come back in now, Harry. Parker will never put his trust in either of us again. This was our one shot. And we blew it."

"Then we'll have no choice but to find him and take him by force."

David glanced over at Zegers. The stern look in the agent's eyes let David know he was dead serious. And although David understood the man's line of thinking, it didn't sit well. Until Zegers found his leak, David could not allow the FBI to get anywhere near Parker again. He'd tried that, and it miserably failed. The only chance David now had at helping Parker was to solve this case himself. David and Jess had to somehow put the pieces together in a way where the FBI would no longer need the boy's testimony. If David could offer that to Parker, maybe he could still save him. But he kept these thoughts to himself. He didn't feel like getting into it with Zegers right now.

"You going to be okay, man?" Zegers asked him.

David felt the tone of the question suggested it was coming more from a friend than an FBI agent. David had to admit, he'd kind of grown to like Zegers, in spite of their hostile beginning. While David questioned many of the man's bulldog tactics, it was clear to him that Zegers was passionate about the job and wanted to do the right thing.

"I don't know," David said. "First, Jess nearly gets run down, and now this. The deeper I go with this case, the more people get hurt."

Zegers perked up. "Wait. What happened to Jess?"

"A few hours ago, some guy in a Camaro tried to take her out on this same street."

Zegers forehead tensed. "A Camaro?"

"Yeah. Barely missed her. But put a friend of mine in the hospital."

"What color?" Zegers asked with a surprising sense of urgency.

"The car?"

"Yes, what color was the Camaro?"

"Yellow, I think."

Zegers cursed. "Did the police arrest the driver?"

"No, he took off. A hit-and-run."

"But you believe it's connected to Parker?"

"Maybe. Jess seems sure of it. She thinks she recognized the driver from a bar where she was asking questions earlier."

"What bar?"

"A place called the Burping Goat. Jess was there to talk with the owner. A guy named Dilly Dyson. We think he might have something to do with all of this."

Zegers ran both hands through his air, then cursed again. Something had clearly rattled the man. Zegers face showed the type of panic David had never seen from the agent. Not even in the aftermath of what had just happened with the rooftop sniper.

"What's going on, Harry?"

"My son was picked up today by someone driving a yellow Camaro."

David's mouth dropped open. "No way."

Zegers suddenly bolted for the door. "I've gotta go. I'll call you later."

THIRTY-EIGHT

After leaving his office, David stopped by to see Rebel, but his friend had unfortunately not seen Parker since they'd left earlier. Then he drove north and found Jess waiting for him in the dark at a small neighborhood park. It was late, and there were no lights, so no one else was in the park. Spotting his approach, Jess immediately jumped from a swing, ran over to him, and wrapped her arms around his neck. He'd called her on the drive over to give her the awful update on where things now stood with Parker.

"I'm so sorry, David. I just can't believe it."

David had to admit her embrace felt good. He was so vulnerable right now and desperately wanted someone to hold him. He pulled her in even closer, his arms snug around her waist. She didn't resist. Their bodies eased into each other in a way where David felt like it could go somewhere else fast if he didn't pull out of it soon. Maybe it was just the intense emotions of it all. For both of them. Each had just survived near-death experiences. He was an emotional train wreck right now and couldn't trust any of his own feelings. And now was unfortunately not the time to explore what felt like a growing chemistry between the two of them.

He took a step back. "I failed him, Jess. I must've told him to *trust me* ten times leading up to what just happened."

"You can't blame yourself." She tilted her head, touched his cheek. "Is this—"

"Blood," he answered, realizing he still hadn't cleaned his face.

"Are you hurt?"

He shook his head. "No, I'm okay. It's not my blood. I was standing right next to one of the agents when he took a direct shot. That guy is going to be okay. But another agent might not make it. He threw his body in front of Parker and probably saved his life. Before the boy ran off."

Jess's shoulders sagged. "That's so awful."

"A complete catastrophe."

"Did they get the shooter?"

"No, he's still on the loose."

"Do you think it could be Richie Maylor?"

He shrugged. "I don't know. But Zegers thinks the same guy who tried to run you over may have taken his son this afternoon."

Jess's eyes widened. "What?"

"He said someone in a yellow Camaro picked up his son after school. He initially believed his boy was simply hanging with the wrong crowd. But now he thinks it could be connected to this case."

"What a terrible thought. I hope he's wrong."

"Me, too. And to make matters even worse, Jess, I think someone on Zegers's team is in on it. There's no other way to explain what just happened. The shooter was planted on a rooftop waiting to ambush us."

She bit her bottom lip. "So what do we do?"

"If we can solve this case ourselves, maybe I can still save Parker."

Her eyebrows pinched. "Because he would no longer need to testify?"

"Right. But if we don't solve it, there's no telling what might happen to that kid. He's never going to turn himself in voluntarily now."

"Then we'd better solve it."

He pitched his head slightly. "Listen, Jess, you don't have to do this with me. This is certainly not what you signed up for when you came walking into my office. There'd be no shame in stepping away. You've already survived one deadly encounter. I don't expect you to keep putting yourself in harm's way because of some stupid court order."

She gave him a playful frown. "You're cute. How long have you been practicing that dumb little speech?"

A tiny grin touched his lips. "The whole drive up. But I do mean it."

"Well, nice try, but I'm not going anywhere. Someone has to stand in the gap for that boy. Plus, I owe it to Bobby Lee to see this thing all the way through now. *And* I think I may have a serious lead on something."

"Tell me."

She pulled out her phone and showed him photos of a man and a woman passionately kissing in the back doorway of a house. "I followed Dyson into this neighborhood from his bar. He drove to a house just around the block from here where he met this woman."

"Who is she?" he asked.

"Max Legley's wife."

David looked up at her with a wrinkled brow. "Are you serious? The dead federal witness's wife?"

"Yes. Get this—it turns out the two of them have been having an affair for at least the past six months."

"How do you know that?"

"I spoke with that same bartender at Dyson's bar a few minutes ago, and he told me his boss started bringing her around back in the spring. He didn't know much about the woman other than she went by Christy and was clearly his boss's latest fling. He said the two of them were private about it but not that private. Christina Legley would even come hang out at the bar sometimes without Dyson. When she'd had too much to drink one night, she told the bartender that her husband was an abusive cheater who constantly threatened to ruin her financially if she ever left him, *and* she wished he was dead."

"Damn. A bartender told you all of that?"

"Yes."

Dave gave her a quizzical look, waiting for further explanation.

"Don't ask," Jess said with a small grin. "I have my ways."

"I'm sure you do." David rubbed his chin, tried to process this new information. "So what if the death of Max Legley has nothing to do with Rick Kingston and the federal fraud case? What if all of that was just used as a smoke screen? I mean, we have a rich wife here who wishes her cheating husband was dead having an ongoing affair with a businessman who's in dire financial straits and desperately trying to save his bar from closing."

Jess twisted up her mouth. "You think in the throes of their affair, they both saw a golden opportunity to help each other out of their own difficulties?"

"Perhaps—if they were willing to kill to do it."

"Which would mean Christina Legley intentionally lied to the FBI. She claimed her husband felt like they were in danger because Kingston had previously said he knew a guy who would kill someone for them."

"Right. Don't you find it odd that they never voiced any concern for their own safety to the feds *before* Legley's death?"

"I certainly do now. But it is a great cover. She really sold it."

"And maybe they would've gotten away with it had Parker not been sleeping in the park that night."

They both took a moment to consider the weight of what suddenly felt like a plausible theory.

"It's still mostly supposition," Jess offered.

He nodded. "We definitely need something more to put a stamp on it."

"So what do we do?"

David sighed, considered that. "Is Dyson still at her house?"

"Yes."

"Then let's watch and wait. See what Dyson does next."

"I'll watch and wait," Jess suggested. "You go find Parker."

David agreed. Both of them didn't need to be sitting in a car outside Christina Legley's house. He'd go stir-crazy knowing Parker could still be hiding somewhere near his office building.

"Okay, call me if anything happens."

THIRTY-NINE

Parker poked his head around the corner of a brick building and closely watched the front entrance of the downtown restaurant. He figured it was pricey because of the way people were dressed and the types of cars in which they were arriving. Mercedes, Lexus, BMW. He already knew what he had to do. He was getting out of town as fast as possible. And not just to the next city over from Austin. He had to go much farther if he had any chance of disappearing from both the FBI and whatever men wanted him dead. No one could be trusted. Not even Mr. Adams. Parker was on his own for the rest of his life—so he'd better get used to it. He was going to Mexico. And the only way for him to get to the border tonight was by somehow stealing a car and driving himself there. No easy task—but he had a plan in mind.

Parker swallowed, tried not to think about what had just happened several blocks over. His sweatshirt hoodie had been completely soaked in blood from the FBI agent who'd gotten shot while throwing him to the ground. So Parker had tossed it into a trash can. But now he was freezing in only his T-shirt and jeans. He rubbed his skinny arms, tried to warm himself, but it wasn't helping much.

His eyes went back to the valet stand, where two guys were scrambling back and forth to a lot two blocks over from the restaurant, parking and retrieving cars for the diners. Parker wondered if the luxury cars would be too fancy for him to figure out how to drive. The old truck at Judd's grandpa's ranch did not have lots of dials, switches, or touch screens. There was no computer in the truck, either. It was stiff and rigid but straightforward. Then again, maybe these cars were so fancy, they would be even easier for him to drive—maybe they'd drive themselves.

There was only one way to find out.

Parker eased away from the building and walked down the sidewalk to get closer to the valet station. Both valet guys wore the same dark-blue shirts with some kind of parking logo on the front. One guy had bushy brown hair; the other had short blond hair. They looked like college students. The valets were trying hard to keep up, but the restaurant seemed busy tonight. Parker inched closer until he was pressed up against the building just ten feet away from the valet stand. Several nicely dressed people were leaving the restaurant and waiting for their cars to arrive. So it was easy for Parker to kind of blend in with everyone out on the sidewalk.

A black Lexus sedan pulled up to the curb in front of the valet station. An older man in a suit and a woman in a pretty dress got out, handed their key fob to the bushy-haired valet, got a ticket, and walked inside. Parker was carefully watching how everything was tagged and where the two valets put the key fobs—on a rack of small hooks inside the valet stand. They did not lock up the rack because they were so busy. The bushy-haired valet jumped into the Lexus sedan, drove up the street, and took a right. Parker had already scoped out the parking lot next door. The blond valet arrived with a fancy SUV for a family. Seconds later, Parker noticed the bushy-haired valet run up the sidewalk, back to the valet stand.

Parker's eyes narrowed, watched exactly where the valet placed the key fob. He kept his eyes locked on the spot while the bushy-haired valet gave out another ticket and jumped back into a car. At the moment, neither valet was at the booth. One was out taking a car, the other, picking up a car. Parker knew he had to move right now if he was going to do this. He started to tense up but then pushed the fear aside. He was done being afraid. He was ready to get his life back on his own terms.

Parker moved to the valet stand. Arriving, he took a quick glance down the sidewalk. No valets in sight. He scanned the front doors. No diners giving him a second look. Reaching inside the stand, Parker grabbed the key fob to the Lexus, shoved it into his jean pocket, and then hit the sidewalk at full speed. Within seconds, he crossed paths with the blond valet. At the street corner, Parker took a sharp right and started running. He turned one more street corner and spotted the valet parking lot. His eyes quickly skimmed the four rows until he spotted the black Lexus sedan in the second row.

Rushing forward into the lot, Parker hit the "Unlock" button on the key fob. The lights on the Lexus blinked. Within seconds, he had the front door open, dropped inside the luxury vehicle, and shut the door behind him. The black leather car seat was way too far back for him to reach the pedals. He found the buttons that moved the seat around and pressed one until the seat was as far forward as possible. Another button raised him up to see over the steering wheel. Parker was relieved when he could both reach the pedals and see through the windshield enough to drive.

He put his hands on the steering wheel, felt his heart pumping nearly as fast as it had been when he was running away from the shooting a few minutes ago. Headlights from another car suddenly flashed right in front of him. Parker ducked down out of the way, hoping he wasn't spotted by one of the valets. He waited a moment and then poked his head back up. The bushy-haired valet parked a Toyota SUV in the row directly in front of him. The guy jumped out and took off running again.

Parker put his foot on the brake, pressed the button on the dash, and the car started right up. Mr. Bidwell used to have a Mercedes that started up in this same way. The headlights immediately popped on. Parker knew he had to get out of there right away, or he'd get busted. Reaching down, he tried to shift the car into drive, but it wouldn't budge. He began to panic. Come on! Then he realized he needed to push the brake down to shift gears. He'd forgotten about that. Pressing the brake, he shifted into drive and eased his foot onto the gas pedal. The car jerked forward, startling Parker. The gas pedal was more sensitive than the one in the old truck on the ranch. He pressed down on the pedal again a little smoother, and the car began moving.

Using the steering wheel, Parker turned into the row and headed toward the exit. He reached the street and put his foot on the brake as cars moved past in front of him. Come on! Come on! Finally, traffic cleared. Parker pushed the gas pedal again and slowly drifted into the actual street. He made the turn just before a speedy little car moved in behind him. Parker tried to look in all the mirrors. Right behind the little car, he noticed another fancy SUV pull into the valet parking lot. Behind the wheel was the blond valet. Parker kept watching the mirror, driving really slowly, wondering if one of the valets would notice the missing Lexus. He wasn't sure what he'd do if the blond came sprinting out, looking all around. Would he press down the gas pedal and just go for it? Or pull over somewhere and start running?

Thankfully, he didn't have to do either. In his mirror, he spotted the blond valet on the sidewalk, hurrying back toward the restaurant—business as usual. The little car behind him was getting annoyed at his slow driving. When it got a chance, the driver of that car whipped around him while honking his horn and giving him a dirty look. Parker actually welcomed a dirty look over a suspicious one. He hadn't thought about how other drivers would react if they saw a twelve-year-old boy driving a Lexus.

Three blocks from the restaurant, Parker pulled over into a parking lot next to a construction site. He needed to get his bearings now that he actually had a vehicle. Searching the dashboard, he found the gas gauge. He was immediately relieved to see the gas tank nearly full. He had no money to put gas in the car. The digital gas gauge said he had 322 miles until empty. Parker's eyes drifted over to the bright touch screen in the middle of the dashboard. He pressed the "Map" button, and the whole screen became a map of where he was in Austin. At the bottom was a box for him to type in his destination. Parker was unsure where exactly was the closest place to get into Mexico, so he simply typed *Mexico border*. Several routes immediately popped up on the screen, taking him down different highways toward Mexico. Parker pressed his finger on the shortest route.

Laredo: 253 miles. Three hours, forty-seven minutes.

Before leaving the parking lot, Parker tried out all the turn signals and buttons. He didn't want to have to be searching out on the highway. When he felt like he had enough of a grasp of how the car worked, he swallowed the lump in his throat and shifted back into drive. He waited for a big gap of space and then pulled back onto the street. Following the map, he found his way onto the feeder road of I-35 within a few blocks. Cars were beginning to race past him now as they merged on to the interstate on-ramp. Parker knew he had to find the courage to drive much faster. He pressed his foot down harder, felt the car pick up speed. Forty. Forty-five. Fifty. Fifty-five. With every incremental increase, he felt his heart beat faster. He'd never driven the truck on the ranch above thirty miles per hour. He was already double that.

He followed another car onto the interstate and within seconds found himself in the far-right lane of a busy highway with an 18-wheeler rumbling in the lane beside him. Parker was gripping the steering wheel so tightly, his hands were quickly becoming numb. Realizing he was holding his breath, he exhaled and loosened his grasp on the wheel. He allowed the 18-wheeler to move past him.

Parker stayed in the right-hand lane. He had no desire to try to shift in and out of multiple lanes on the highway. He would stay put right where he was for as long as possible. Fortunately, the map on the bright screen told him he never even needed to leave I-35. The long highway would take him straight to the border in Laredo.

With each mile that passed, Parker began to relax a bit more.

He could do this. No, he was *going* to do this.

The map said only 241 miles to go.

FORTY

From the front seat of his Jeep Wrangler, Zegers stared across the street at a small one-story gray-brick house sandwiched in a neighborhood of nearly matching homes. His heart hadn't stopped racing since David had told him about the yellow Camaro earlier—a car that he now spotted sitting in the driveway in front of him. Josh had been picked up earlier from school in an unidentified yellow Camaro. Zegers's gut said it was no coincidence. Someone had grabbed his son. Why? Could whoever was behind the hit on the federal witness be planning to use his son to influence the investigation somehow?

Zegers again thought about having a potential traitor on his team. Could whoever had leaked info about their meeting with Parker earlier tonight also been willing to betray him and his family? He felt his stomach turn over in rage. He now planned to put every member of his crew who'd been involved with this investigation into a holding room, where he was going to have a very intense one-on-one conversation.

But first things first. He had to get his son back.

After leaving David's office earlier, Zegers had immediately contacted the Austin Police Department and asked to speak with the detective handling the downtown hit-and-run incident from earlier tonight. The detective was already off duty but told him over the phone they had a lead but hadn't found the guy yet. A downtown security camera had captured the incident and revealed a license plate. The car was registered to someone named Luke Detrich. The detective said he'd sent officers by Detrich's home earlier but found no one there. He had an officer waiting outside in case the suspect returned.

Of course, Zegers was not waiting around. He immediately began his own investigation and was able to identify several addresses for Detrich's local family members. For the past hour, Zegers had been driving all over town, looking for a yellow Camaro with black racing stripes. It was tedious work to do all by himself, but he was unwilling to bring anyone else from his team into the fold at this point. He couldn't take any chances. Not with his son's well-being on the line. He'd finally found the Camaro a few minutes ago sitting outside a house being rented by one of Detrich's cousins.

Zegers looked down when his phone buzzed. Mark Anderson. The assistant US attorney had been incessantly calling him for the past hour, wanting an update. He'd obviously heard about the screwup downtown and was going to give Zegers hell about it. Zegers kept pushing "Ignore." He didn't feel like dealing with the man's yapping at the moment. When his phone immediately buzzed again—once again showing Anderson's name—Zegers finally turned his phone off.

He turned his attention back to the house. Sitting beside the Camaro was a small white Toyota truck. The grass in the yard was taller than other yards, and weeds were poking through the cracks in the driveway. Zegers couldn't see inside any of the front windows. All the blinds and curtains had been pulled. But he could tell lights were on inside the house. Someone was inside. But would he find Josh?

Getting out of his car, Zegers drew his gun. He moved across the street and up the sidewalk to the driveway. A quick inspection of the Camaro showed dents across the hood and cracks in the windshield. He stood in the driveway for only a moment, considering his options. It was probably most appropriate to knock on the front door and identify himself as FBI.

But he didn't care about proper protocol right now. And he certainly wasn't interested in giving anyone inside a heads-up.

Zegers moved to the front door. The front light was either not on or burned out. Either way, he was grateful to approach in the dark. He wondered if he'd have to kick the door open or even shoot out the lock. Gun in his right hand, he reached down with his left to the door handle. The door clicked open. No need to kick or shoot.

He slowly pushed the door open a few inches. He could now hear music blaring from somewhere in the back of the house. Sounded like some kind of heavy metal–punk rock mix. Slipping inside the entryway, Zegers shut the door behind him. To his right was a small dining room with what looked like antique furniture. No one was in the room. A hallway straight ahead led to the rest of the small house. Zegers saw a shadow of movement down the hallway and stretched out the gun in both hands in front of him. He took a few deep breaths to calm himself.

He moved deeper into the hallway, passed by a bathroom on one side and a closet on the other. He could tell the hallway led into a kitchen and living room just up ahead. The music was already giving him a headache. A young guy suddenly crossed from the living room into the kitchen just ahead of him. He didn't notice Zegers. The skinny guy had long brown hair, wore jeans, and was bare-chested. A second later, Zegers heard, "We need more beer" from a deep voice in the living room.

There were at least two people here. Were there others?

Zegers peeked into the living room, quickly surveyed the area. A muscle-bound guy with a crew cut sat on a leather sofa. He matched what Zegers had found online for Luke Detrich. The man wore a tight black T-shirt and jeans. Zegers saw a gun sitting on the coffee table in front of him. There was also drug paraphernalia on the table. Looked like heroin. Zegers peered toward the back of the living room and spotted a hallway that led to bedrooms. If his son was in the house, he had to be back there somewhere.

Taking another breath, Zegers exhaled and moved fully into the living room. He charged right up to the muscle-bound guy and aimed his gun at the guy's forehead. The guy suddenly realized what was happening and glanced over at his own gun on the table.

"FBI!" Zegers yelled. "Don't move, or I'll literally blow your damn head off."

From behind him, Zegers heard, "Dude, what the—"

Zegers spun around, aimed, fired his gun. The bullet shattered a beer bottle the young guy was holding in his right hand. The guy yanked his hand back. Zegers pivoted to the other man, who was stupidly leaning in toward the coffee table. Instead of shooting him, since Zegers might need information from the guy, he kicked him in the face as hard as he could. The man's head whipped back, and he fell into the couch. By the cracking sound, Zegers was sure he'd broken his nose. The man immediately put both hands to his face, where blood was beginning to gush.

Zegers turned again to the skinny guy. "On the couch! Now!"

The skinny guy put both hands up in a surrendering posture, hurried into the living room, and sat next to the other one. Zegers kept pointing his gun back and forth between the two men. The skinny guy looked scared out of his mind.

"Is the kid here?" Zegers said.

"What kid?" the bigger guy replied, blood seeping down into his mouth.

Zegers shifted his aim, fired his gun. It hit the big guy in his left kneecap. He yelled out in pain. Zegers then aimed directly at the skinny guy's knee. He folded easily. He again held up both hands.

"Please, no—don't shoot me, man. The kid is here. He's in the back bedroom."

"Show me," Zegers commanded.

Zegers reached down, grabbed the gun that was sitting on the coffee table, and shoved it into the back of his pants. The skinny guy hesitantly got up, moved around the table. Zegers glanced at the big guy, who was curled up on the couch, cursing, clutching his right knee, and groaning in pain. Zegers followed the other one into the back hallway. They moved past two bedrooms, and then the guy opened the door to the third bedroom. The light was currently off inside, and the bedroom was silent. Zegers felt a kind of fear he'd never experienced before move through his whole body. Was Josh okay?

He shoved the skinny guy into the bedroom, keeping him in front of him, and then turned on the bedroom light. Josh was sitting on the carpet in the corner, his hands and feet bound by duct tape, his mouth covered with a strip of tape. The sight of his son was both relieving and terrifying. But the boy's eyes lit up upon seeing his father.

Zegers pushed the skinny guy into an opposite corner and then rushed over to his son. He quickly tore the tape off his mouth.

"Dad!" Josh called out.

"It's okay, I'm here."

Zegers quickly unfastened the boy's feet and hands, then pulled him up from the carpet. He hugged him tightly.

Zegers glared at the skinny guy. "Who did this? Who hired you?"

"I don't know, man. I swear, I don't know anything. Luke made me do it."

Zegers forced him back into the living room, where the bigger guy had fallen onto the carpet, still holding his knee, blood pooling around him. He would need a medic but not before Zegers had a chance to interrogate him. He had to get answers. He had to find out who put him up to this.

Turning to his son, Zegers said, "Josh, go straight out the front door. My Jeep is parked to the right up the street. Get in, and wait for me there. I'll be out in a few minutes."

"But Dad—"

"Do it!"

Zegers didn't want his son around to see him beat information out of this guy. Josh turned and rushed down the hallway toward the front door. But when he opened it, Zegers spotted a police officer quickly approaching up the sidewalk. He cursed. A neighbor must've called the police upon hearing the gunshots. Zegers knew he'd unfortunately now have to wait until the wounded man got medical attention before he'd be able to interrogate him. Pulling out his FBI credentials, Zegers moved to the front door to speak with the officer himself and begin to clear up the matter. As he did, Zegers took a deep breath and let it out slowly. His son was safe.

And that was all that really mattered right now.

FORTY-ONE

Parker was completely exhausted when he finally pulled the Lexus sedan into a truck stop called the Pilot Travel Center just a mile from the Texas-Mexico border. Not only was he going on hardly any sleep for the past couple of nights, but his nerves were shot from driving all night in the right lane as other cars constantly buzzed by him. Several times he nearly pulled over onto the shoulder to try to calm himself but then somehow found the resolve to keep going. He parked the Lexus in the back of the truck stop near a long row of 18-wheelers all lined up together. The digital clock on the dash said 1:32. In many ways, Parker couldn't believe he'd actually made it all the way from Austin to Laredo.

He was almost to freedom.

But he had to pee so bad, he thought his eyeballs must be yellow.

He got out of the car, shut the door behind him. He'd parked away from other cars so no one would notice a kid like him getting out of a fancy Lexus. He wondered if the car had already been reported stolen. He was sure it had to be by now. It must've been quite the scene back at the restaurant when the valets couldn't find the older couple's vehicle. Not that Parker enjoyed that thought. He didn't want to get anyone in trouble. The whole drive down, he'd feared that a police car would suddenly pull up behind him with the lights flashing. Not because he was speeding—he hadn't gone more than one mile per hour over the speed limit the entire drive—but because an officer had spotted the license plate of a car that had been reported stolen. Parker had never prayed so hard.

Hopefully, the older couple would get the car back soon once it was discovered in the parking lot of this truck stop. Parker had no plans to use it anymore. He knew he couldn't drive straight across the border. From watching movies, he remembered the border had checkpoints where people looked at your driver's license or passport or something like that. None of which Parker had, of course. He'd have to figure out another way to get across.

But first, he had to pee.

Walking around the corner of the building, Parker found the glass front doors to the massive truck stop. The place had row after row of food, snacks, clothes, and even toys. There was also a restaurant. The truck stop was surprisingly busy, with various truckers and other folks grabbing something to eat or drink or just taking a break. Spotting a huge sign in the corner that said **RESTROOM & SHOWERS**, Parker made his way through the aisles and hustled into the restrooms. There were probably about twenty standing urinals with an equal number of private stalls. Moving to the first available urinal, Parker quickly relieved himself and felt so much better.

After washing his hands, he poked his head inside a hallway with private showers on one side and small bunkrooms on the other. He guessed the bunkrooms were so the truck drivers could catch a quick nap before hitting the road again—if they didn't have the kind of truck with its own bed. There was a guy in the first bunkroom, but the second was empty. Stepping inside, Parker shut the door behind him, then sat on the bottom bunk. He needed somewhere to think for a moment, anyway. This seemed like a good spot. The bed had pretty decent covers on it.

He scooted himself all the way back against the wall and pulled out the phone Mr. Adams had given him back in Austin. On the drive down, he'd remembered he had it and thought he might be able to use it to search the internet on how to get himself across the border.

For a second, Parker thought about Mr. Adams, and sadness tugged at him. The man was probably worried sick. Parker had no idea what had happened with the FBI and the shooting earlier, but he didn't figure it was Mr. Adams's fault. Still, Parker knew he couldn't reach out to him again. It was too dangerous. He'd tried that once, and it had backfired. And it nearly got both him and Mr. Adams shot. He had no idea what awaited him in Mexico, but he just knew it had to be better than what all he'd been through the past week.

Parker turned on the phone, found the web browser icon, and opened it up. Using Google, he began searching and scanning.

What do you need to get across Mexico border?

Can a kid cross border alone?

Do police search 18-wheelers at the border?

Can you stow away across the border?

Sitting there reading on the phone, Parker's eyelids became heavy. The bunk bed was comfortable. He lay down and held the phone up above him as he continued to try to read. But he didn't last very long. He couldn't keep his eyes open. Maybe it would be best for him to catch a quick nap, anyway. He probably had a long journey ahead of him, and the rest would help him think more clearly. He set the phone down beside him on the bed and closed his eyes.

Within seconds, he was dead asleep.

FORTY-TWO

David zipped his jacket up to his neck. It became colder as the night wore on. He put his hands in his pockets, turned a street corner, moved up another downtown sidewalk. He'd been walking the blocks all around his office building for the past hour, hoping to spot something that might lead him to finding Parker. But so far, nothing. He needed sleep but knew that wouldn't be possible at this point. Not with Parker out there scared and alone. David couldn't possibly imagine what kind of emotional condition the boy was in right now. He pulled his phone out again, like he'd been doing every ten minutes since Parker had bolted on him, and checked the Find My Phone app to see if Parker had finally turned on the phone he'd given him earlier. David had lost hope a long time ago. Still, he kept checking.

Clicking on the app, he gave it a glance and nearly closed out of it just out of habit. But then his eyes widened. He pulled it closer. On the screen was a phone listed as OFFICE PHONE. David couldn't believe it. That was the name of the phone he'd given Parker. He clicked on the name and watched a map begin to form on the screen. David cursed. The map showed the city of Laredo. He zoomed in as far as he could and found the dot showing the phone at a truck stop called the

Pilot Travel Center near the Mexican border. David felt his jaw drop. Was this possible? Could Parker actually be in Laredo? But how would Parker have even gotten to the border? David couldn't wrap his mind around it.

He immediately placed a call to the phone. Come on, kid, please pick up! Please! But it rang four times and went to an automated voice mail. He called it right back but got the same result. Could Parker see he was calling and was simply ignoring him? David decided to text instead. Parker, it's David Adams. Please call me back ASAP. I can still help you. Please call me!

David held his phone close to his eyes to see if he could spot the little dots on the screen that showed someone was replying to his message. But no dots ever appeared. David's thoughts were spinning in different directions. If Parker was truly trying to get across the border—and that certainly appeared to be the case—David needed to try to stop him. Mexico was no place for a twelve-year-old kid to go and hide. David had hoped to wait until he and Jess had put a bow on their theory about Christina Legley and Dilly Dyson to call Zegers back. But with Parker at the border, David needed help. He had to stop the boy from doing something really stupid. Even if he didn't trust the FBI right now, David knew Zegers could probably have agents at the border within minutes.

Feeling desperate, David called Zegers's phone. It immediately went to voice mail. He called right back. Same thing. Come on, Harry, answer! A third call had the same results. David left a frantic voice mail. "Harry, David here. I found Parker. I need your help, man. I'm trusting you despite everything that's happened today. Please don't let me down. You won't believe this, but somehow the kid is in Laredo. I have no idea how he got there. But from what I can tell, he's about a mile from the border at a place called the Pilot Travel Center. Harry, I think the kid is going to try to cross into Mexico. We can't let him do that. Call me back ASAP!"

Hanging up, David considered what he should do next. If and when the FBI took Parker into custody, the kid would freak out. David needed to be there with him as soon as possible to help calm him down and reassure him that everything was going to be okay. And there was only one way to do that at two in the morning.

He needed to get in his damn truck and start driving.

FORTY-THREE

Jess was surprised to see Dilly Dyson on the move because she'd just gotten off the phone with David and received the full update about Parker. Coincidence? Her gut didn't believe so, which made her really uneasy. Where was the man going at two thirty in the morning? From her perch in the driver's seat of her Ford Explorer just down the street from the house, she watched as the bar owner quickly hustled down the driveway and jumped into his Mercedes. There was nothing casual about the way the man was moving—he clearly wasn't just headed back to his own place for the rest of the night. Something was up.

Jess followed at a safe distance. She had to do her best driving to keep up with Dyson without him noticing he had a tail. It was tricky. He was driving fast, and there wasn't much other traffic out on the streets that allowed her to easily blend in behind him. If she lost him, it wouldn't be the end of the world. She'd attached a tiny GPS tracking device the size of a quarter underneath the carriage of his car that she could monitor with an app on her phone. She had all kinds of tools like this in her bag because she never knew what all she'd need in her job as an investigator. But she didn't want to chance something messing up with the tracking device or the app.

With each turn, Dyson seemed to get a heavier foot. This was much different from the way he'd driven over to Christina Legley's house earlier. Again, the timing was unsettling. Could his abrupt departure have something to do with Parker? David was a nervous wreck because he'd not heard back from Zegers.

Dyson was headed downtown. It was easier for Jess to follow once they both got up onto the highway. Dyson didn't seem to care if he got a ticket as he had his Mercedes up over ninety now. Jess did the same and hoped her Explorer's engine wouldn't fall apart on her. Dyson exited the highway at Fifteenth and took the street into downtown. Twice Jess had to run a red light so she wouldn't lose him. Her adrenaline was really starting to spike.

Minutes later, Dyson pulled his Mercedes to the curb along Red River Street, right outside the Dell Seton Medical Center. It was the same hospital where Bobby Lee was currently recovering. Why was Dyson coming here? Jess pulled to the curb on the opposite side of the street. She squinted across the way at the Mercedes. Dyson was not getting out. What was he doing? Pulling out her phone, Jess used her camera to zoom in as close as possible. It looked like Dyson was typing on his phone. Maybe sending a text to someone? She obviously couldn't tell from her vantage point. She watched, waited. She had her answer a few seconds later, and it made her curse out loud. Agent Farley appeared on the sidewalk outside the hospital, carefully looked both ways, and then made his way over to Dyson's Mercedes. Jess held up her phone, began taking photos. Was Farley the traitor? The FBI insider who had been passing along information?

Dyson rolled down his window, and Farley leaned into it. Jess quickly pulled up the GPS tracking app for the device she'd attached under the carriage of the car behind the front left tire. The device also had live audio monitoring. She hoped it was within range to catch whatever the two men were about to say to each other. She turned the volume all the way up. It worked. She could hear both men plain as day.

"This is the last time I do this," Farley said.

"You'll be square when this is over. That was the agreement."

"But this has spiraled way out of control."

"As did your gambling debt. So unless you're about to hand me sixty thousand dollars, you'll finish what you started."

Farley sighed. "Why the hell did you grab Zegers's son?"

"Leverage. If it came down to it, I planned to offer a swap. Your boss's kid for the Barnes kid."

"Well, it didn't work."

"No, it unfortunately did not."

"Will your boy with the Camaro talk to the police?"

"No, Luke has a little sister he adores. He knows what'll happen to her if he says anything to the police. What do you got for me?"

Jess watched as Farley handed Dyson what looked like a scrap of paper.

"This is the exact location for the kid."

Dyson stared at the paper. "How did you get this?"

"The attorney called Zegers and left a voice mail."

"You bugged your boss's phone?"

Farley nodded. "I'm not proud of it."

"You think the boy's actually trying to run away to Mexico?"

"Why the hell else would he go there, Dilly?"

Dyson shook his head. "This stupid kid is like a damn mouse we can't seem to catch, no matter how many traps we set."

"Maybe you should just let him go?" Farley offered. "If he gets across the border, I doubt we'll keep searching for him."

"Is the FBI already on their way to grab him?"

"No, my boss hasn't checked his voice mail yet."

"That's good." Dyson took a moment, then said, "I can't risk letting the kid go. He needs to be permanently shut up, or he'll always be a threat. I'll get Richie on the road ASAP. Do whatever you can to delay."

"Fine. But finish this already."

At that, Farley stepped away from the vehicle and went back inside the hospital. Dyson rolled up his window and then jumped on his phone. Because the tracking device was outside the car, Jess couldn't hear whatever conversation he had next. But she already knew. Dyson was sending Richie Maylor to the border.

Jess immediately called David.

"Where are you?" she asked.

"Not far. A few miles outside of Austin. Why?"

"Drive fast, David. Parker is in real trouble."

"I know . . . What do you—"

"No, I mean serious trouble. It's Agent Farley, David! He's the one feeding them inside info. Dyson just met with him outside Dell Seton!"

David cursed. "Farley?"

"Yes. Listen to this conversation I just recorded."

On her tracking app, Jess replayed the conversation between Farley and Dyson so David could hear it over the phone.

"How did you get that, Jess?"

"I attached a tracking device to Dyson's car. They just had this conversation right outside of the hospital."

"Damn it, Jess. I led those guys straight to him."

"Is Parker still in the same spot?"

"Yes, according to my app. But he still won't answer the phone or reply to any of my texts. And my damn phone is about to die on me!"

"What do you want me to do?"

David sighed. "Call the police in Laredo. Tell them we have reason to believe a boy is in danger. Give them the location of the travel center. See if we can get lucky. Then you've got to somehow get to Zegers and tell him everything."

"What are you going to do?"
"Race them to Laredo. Try to—"
There was sudden silence on the phone.
"David?" Jess said.
She held her phone away from her ear. David was gone.
Which meant his phone was dead.

FORTY-FOUR

David tossed his dead phone onto the passenger seat. For a moment, he considered trying to pull off somewhere to find a gas station that might sell a portable car charger. But he knew he'd lose valuable time on the highway doing that. Right now, he had a brief lead on Richie Maylor. If he stopped, he'd likely lose that lead. He couldn't risk that. Besides, Parker was not responding to any of his calls or texts. The smartest thing he could do was keep driving, so he pressed his foot down harder on the gas.

The old Chevy truck was only capable of a certain high-end speed. He couldn't chance blowing out the engine, no matter how fast he wanted to go right now. At some point, he would also have to pull off and get gas. He only had half a tank. That was frustrating. His mind went to Agent Farley. He couldn't believe it. Zegers had seemed to trust him more than any other agent. The recorded conversation made it sound like Dyson had failed in using Zegers's son as leverage. He hoped that meant the boy was okay.

David squeezed the steering wheel in tight fists and weaved around a slow-moving SUV. David didn't know what to expect when Jess called the police in Laredo. Would they even take her seriously? He figured they would at least send a car over to check it out. But how was one lone cop going to find and secure Parker when the FBI couldn't? Still, they had to do something. He couldn't chance that Dyson might know someone else in Laredo whom he would try to send over to get to Parker.

David zipped around three more cars. His truck was really moving now. He couldn't believe he was racing down the highway to the border in the middle of the night in one last desperate attempt to save Parker Barnes. How had it come to this? But he had to get to the boy first. Before, he'd wanted the boy to stay put. Now David wasn't so sure.

Pressing his foot down even farther, David began to feel the old truck vibrate in a way he'd never experienced.

But he didn't slow down. He kept speeding up.

FORTY-FIVE

Zegers rolled onto his left side, his back beginning to ache something fierce. He'd been trying to sleep on a huge beanbag chair in the corner of his son's bedroom. Lisa was curled up in the bed with Josh. Both of them were sound asleep. Upon bringing Josh home earlier, neither Lisa nor Josh wanted him to leave. Truth be told, neither did Zegers. The whole thing with Josh had really scared all of them. In this brief moment, they were a family again. And Zegers wanted to hold on to that feeling for as long as possible. He knew it was fleeting. He and his ex would be fighting again in no time. But not right now. So he stayed.

Zegers squinted over at the digital clock Josh had sitting on the nightstand next to his bed: 5:13. Stretching his back out a little, Zegers tried to get more comfortable in the beanbag chair and go back to sleep. But his back was not allowing it. Instead, he let his mind again run through the events from earlier. The man with the crew cut and the fresh bullet hole in his knee had been arrested. For the moment, he wasn't talking. And unfortunately, the other guy didn't seem to know much. Josh had told Zegers that the crew cut guy approached him right after football practice, claimed he was an FBI agent who worked for his dad, and that Zegers had instructed him to come pick him up. Josh went along with it because his dad had done something like this before when he'd been tied up during an investigation. Josh said he didn't realize something was off until they got to the strange house. He sent a quick text to his mom. But then the crew cut guy grabbed his phone, dragged him inside, bound him with duct tape, and stuck him in that dark bedroom. Zegers planned to interrogate the crew cut guy first thing that morning.

Realizing he was now wide-awake, Zegers found his phone in the pocket of his jacket on the carpet next to him. He powered it back up, expecting a barrage of angry voice mails and text messages from Mark Anderson. His eyes suddenly widened as messages began loading on his phone—including one that had arrived just ten minutes ago from Jess Raven. What the hell?

CALL ME ASAP!!!

Zegers quickly scrolled down and saw a half dozen other text messages over the past couple of hours from Jess, all in the same vein of urgency. Why? Getting up from the floor, Zegers moved out of the bedroom and into the hallway. He quietly shut the door behind him and then dialed Jess's phone. She answered immediately.

"Harry, thank God! Where are you?"

"At my ex's house. What's going on?"

"David found Parker Barnes. The boy is in Laredo. David is driving there right now because Parker is in serious trouble."

"What? Laredo? How do you—"

"Harry, listen to me," Jess interrupted him. "Farley betrayed us."

"Farley? No way. I don't believe—"

"I'm sending something to you right now. I recorded a private encounter between Farley and a man named Dilly Dyson, whom we believe is the mastermind behind this whole thing. Listen to it and call me right back. We've got to get someone to Laredo before it's too late."

Jess hung up. Zegers checked his messages and opened the text that she'd just sent to him. Farley? She must be mistaken. David had mentioned the name Dilly Dyson earlier. The text was an audio file. He pressed "Play" and then listened to a conversation between a voice he clearly recognized as belonging to Farley along with another man. The hair on the back of his neck stood straight up as the shock of betrayal set in on him. His own trusted right-hand man had sold him out. The shock quickly moved to anger and then urgency. Zegers knew he had to move fast.

Stepping back into the bedroom, Zegers gave his son a quick peck on the head and then left. On the way to the front door, he called Jess back.

"Meet me at my office ASAP!"

FORTY-SIX

David pulled into the massive parking lot directly in front of the Pilot Travel Center in Laredo and came to a sudden stop as dust circled around his vehicle. He did a quick scan. Probably two dozen regular gas pumps to his left for standard vehicles. A dozen more gas pumps to his right for 18-wheelers. A long line of the big trucks sat idly behind those pumps. Truckers were coming and going. To the right of the main truck stop building was a row of huge warehouses.

David checked the time. He'd made it as fast as he could. But had he beat Richie Maylor? There was no way to be sure. David had only made one quick stop to pump just enough gas into his tank to ensure that he could get here. No second could be spared. Still, it took him six hectic minutes to do that.

Taking a deep breath, he got out. It was still dark. The sun wouldn't be hitting the horizon for at least another hour. It was much warmer down by the border than back in Austin. Or maybe it was just his nerves pushing sweat down his back. Because his phone was dead, David had no idea if Parker was still on the property. He'd held out a glimmer of hope that the Laredo police might have actually found Parker and taken the boy back to the police station.

David moved toward the front doors of the main building, his eyes bouncing everywhere. Could Richie Maylor have possibly beaten him to the border? He didn't see a truck that looked like Maylor's parked anywhere. Pushing through the doors, David took in the truck stop. It looked like a lot of truckers were getting ready to head out on their long drives for the day. But there was no immediate sign of Parker anywhere out in the open. Not that he expected to find the boy sitting in a restaurant booth, enjoying waffles.

David walked over to a clerk behind one of the front counters. He read the name tag attached to her blue dress. "Hi, Gladys. How are you?"

"Just fine, hon. What can I do for you?"

"I'm an attorney working a case. Strange question, but have you seen a small boy around here? Twelve years old, shaved head, probably wearing a hoodie sweatshirt and blue jeans?"

"No, I haven't. But you're the second to ask me that on my shift."

David hoped the first wasn't Maylor. "Who else came asking?"

"Officer Mickens came by earlier, wondering the same thing."

David exhaled. "He didn't find the boy?"

"No, he did some looking around and then left. What's the deal with this missing boy?"

"We just need to get him home, that's all."

"Well, like I told Gabe, I'll be keeping my eye out."

"Thanks."

David was disappointed but not surprised to hear the news about the police officer not finding Parker. He walked over to his left and began casually searching the restaurant patrons. If a police officer had been here and didn't find Parker, could that mean the boy was already on the move? Had he simply left the phone behind—moved on without it? That was quite possible. David didn't see anyone of interest in the restaurant, so he went back over to the rows of food and goods.

He walked up and down each aisle, then finally headed back into the restrooms. A dozen or so truckers were lined up at the urinals. David counted about twenty private stalls. He began slowly passing by each one, trying to check out shoes underneath without looking like some kind of creep. He reached the end, sighed.

There was still no sign of Parker anywhere.

FORTY-SEVEN

Richie nearly took out a truck driver who was walking back to his rig as he skidded his truck to a stop in the parking lot out front of the truck stop. The trucker gave him a dirty look, and Richie gave him the bird. He then turned to Manny, who was sitting next to him. They had driven as fast as possible to the border city.

"This is the place, right?" he asked Manny.

"Yeah, it's what Dilly gave you."

He glanced at Manny. "You ready?"

"Hell yeah. We didn't drive way the hell down here for nothing."

Richie grabbed his gun off the seat next to him, made sure the suppressor was securely attached, and then shoved it into the front of his jeans. Manny was also armed. His buddy had assured him he had his back—which meant he was also prepared to shoot the kid, if necessary.

Richie knew it was now or never. If he didn't get the kid this time around, he wasn't going back to Austin. He knew what fate awaited him there. Instead, he would jump in his truck, cross the border, and start a new life.

But Richie planned to finish the job.

"Let's go," he said.

FORTY-EIGHT

Parker was startled awake by a bright light. His eyes popped wide-open. For a brief moment, he was disoriented. Where was he? The bottom of a bunk bed? Then he remembered he was in the bunkroom at the truck stop. Why was the light on? He rolled over, tried to look toward the door.

"Oh, sorry, pal," said a gruff voice from the door. "Didn't realize someone was already using this room."

The guy at the door flipped off the light and shut the door fully behind him. Parker rubbed his eyes. He figured it must've been a truck driver looking to lie down and rest for a bit. How long had he been asleep? He felt around him on the bed until his hand came to rest on the phone Mr. Adams had given him earlier. He pressed a button, again felt blinded by the bright light of the phone's screen. The time said 5:28. But that's not where his eyes remained. He immediately spotted notifications of several missed calls and four different text messages from David Adams.

He quickly scanned them.

Please call me, Parker!

I can still make this right. Call me!

You're not safe, Parker! You have to call me back!

Please, Parker! I know it's hard to trust me right now, but I can and will help you. I just need you to call me.

He put the phone down on the bed. Although he felt so badly about it, Parker had no intention of calling Mr. Adams back. The plan was in place, and he felt committed to following through on it. Pushing out of the bed, Parker moved toward the door. It was time to find a ride into Mexico.

He stepped into the hallway and then followed it back into the main store. It was definitely busier now than when he'd gotten there a couple of hours ago. Although he was really hungry, Parker didn't have any money on him. This time he wasn't going to steal to satisfy that need. Not when he was this close to getting his freedom. That would be way too risky. He thought about asking a random trucker to buy him something, but again, he didn't want to draw any unwanted attention to himself. He would just have to starve himself until he was in Mexico and figure it out from there.

Hands in pockets, Parker followed two truck drivers out a side door and trailed them as they headed back to where all the 18-wheelers were parked. One of the drivers peeled off to a black 18-wheeler and paused to check his phone before climbing aboard.

"Hey, mister, you headed into Mexico today?" Parker asked.

The guy turned, examined him. "Nope. Just returned. Why?"

Parker shrugged. "Just curious. Here with my dad, who's inside, and he said I could go check out all the cool trucks."

The guy nodded. "You want to see inside?"

"No, thanks."

Parker moved onto the next truck. He would make his way down the entire line to find out who all was going across the border. Then he'd carefully examine those trucks for potential stowaway locations. Hopefully, he'd be in Mexico before the sun even came up today.

Parker was circling around the back of a gray 18-wheeler in the middle, giving it a good look since the driver said he was about to head into Mexico, when he bumped right into the chest of a man. At first he figured it was just one of the drivers, so he was about to apologize. Then his eyes went up to the man's face, and his whole body locked up with fear.

It was him. The killer. Mr. Adams called him Richie something— and the guy stood right in front of him with his beady eyes peering down into Parker's soul.

"Hey, kid. Your damn luck has finally run out."

Parker turned to run, but the guy immediately grabbed his T-shirt in his left fist and held him.

"Don't make this difficult, you little punk," the guy said.

That's when Parker noticed the gun in the man's right hand. Parker knew he had to do something quick, or he'd shoot him right there. Parker spun back toward the man, raised a knee, and thrust it upward. It caught the guy square between the legs, just as he'd intended. He hunched over in agony, barely able to breathe, but he still wouldn't let go of Parker's shirt. So Parker twisted himself sideways until the shirt pulled right off his body.

Bare-chested now, he ran for it. He heard the now-familiar sound of the gun firing behind him and tensed, expecting to be hit with a bullet, but it ricocheted off the side of the 18-wheeler right in front of him. Parker hit the pavement, rolled to his left underneath the trailer, hoping he was out of the guy's line of sight.

Popping up on the other side, he sprinted to his left, back toward the travel center, when he stopped in his tracks. Directly ahead of him appeared another man who looked familiar. This guy's eyes were also locked directly on him. And that's when Parker remembered him from the parking garage. He'd been with the goateed man.

Spinning, Parker took off running in the opposite direction. He crossed behind another 18-wheeler, then spotted the row of warehouses just across the parking lot.

He paused for only a moment before making a run for them.

FORTY-NINE

Feeling defeated, David stepped outside the front doors of the truck stop. Parker could be long gone by now. The kid could have been there for only a moment, left the phone, and then taken off again. Maybe the boy was already in Mexico. Jess was right—Parker was incredibly resourceful. Maybe the kid could actually make a new life there. Maybe the boy could survive.

David knew he was trying to talk himself into something to help himself feel better, but it wasn't really working. He was about to walk back over to his truck, find his phone, and take it back inside the truck stop to charge it when something off to his left caught his eye. He glanced over toward the row of 18-wheelers all parked side by side. And that's when he saw the shadowy figure of someone running. David knew that figure well. He had seen the same running motion only a few hours earlier as he'd watched Parker race away from the downtown shooting.

It was him. He'd found Parker. But why was the boy running away from the truck stop toward the warehouses next door? David was about to yell out Parker's name when he spotted two men chasing the boy. David cursed. He took off running in the same direction.

It couldn't end this way. He wouldn't let it.

FIFTY

Parker sprinted up to the dark warehouse buildings, looking for some-where—anywhere!—to hide. He couldn't believe he was only one mile away from his freedom in Mexico, and they had found him. He should've never let himself fall asleep. That was so stupid. But how did they find him? How could they have possibly known he was there? He was so confused. All the big garage doors were closed on the first warehouse. He ran up to two regular-size metal doors, but they were both locked. Pivoting, Parker could see the two men quickly crossing the parking lot and making their way toward him.

Turning around, Parker raced up to the next warehouse building. Just then, one of the big garage doors opened and began to slide all the way up. Two trucks were parked out front, and Parker figured workers must be getting the facility up and running for the day. He tucked his head down and ran as hard as he could toward the open garage door. Not even pausing, Parker darted inside. The warehouse was well lit, which he was not too excited about. He spotted a guy with a cap across the way, staring at a clipboard. But the guy didn't notice him. There were probably a dozen two-story metal shelves in the building, all filled with boxes and crates. Parker rushed down the center of one aisle, won-dering how he could get himself lost in here. Maybe if he could hide out long enough while more workers showed up, the guys with the guns would get spooked and go away.

Unlike earlier in the parking garage, where Parker had found the courage to slip away in a front hiding spot, his fear drove his feet all the way to the back wall of the warehouse. Maybe he could find a back door somewhere and slip out. But the row dead-ended into another tall row of shelves filled with crates. Parker peered left, right, then chose right and ran again. Sweat was pouring down his face. He tried to wipe it away with a wet hand. He saw movement off to his right from another row, and it made him pause. Was that one of his pursuers? Or just a worker?

Looking to his left, Parker spotted a crawl space between two huge crates. It was dark back there behind the crates. While it felt more natural to keep running, Parker knew he couldn't do it forever. He had to hide. Getting down on his knees, he slipped in between the crates. One of the crate edges caught his side. Because he had no shirt on, Parker felt it cut into his skin. He grimaced but kept moving all the way behind one of the crates, where he pulled his legs up to his chest. He tried to hold his breath, but he was shaking so much, it was difficult.

After waiting for about ten seconds, he poked his head slightly around the crate to see if anyone was nearby. Someone was—the man with the goatee. And the man's eyes were looking straight into the crack between the two crates at Parker. Then a sinister smile touched the guy's lips.

All Parker could think about in that moment was his mom and dad. He missed them so much every day.

At least he would get to see them again soon.

FIFTY-ONE

David hustled into the warehouse not ten seconds after the two guys who were chasing Parker. He saw no sign of them, so he hit a row in the middle at full speed. He had to again fight the urge to yell Parker's name. If the kid was well hidden, David didn't need to be drawing him out. But where were Richie Maylor and the other guy? David made it to the end of the row and dead-ended into the back wall. He looked left, then right, and that's when he noticed Maylor standing ten feet over from him with his gun raised at something among the crates against the wall.

David felt his heart in his throat. If the target was Parker, it was about to be over. He ran toward Maylor and then hurled himself in the air. The man caught a glimpse of him, began to turn, but it was too late. David tackled Maylor with a strong shoulder right into the man's side, like a linebacker smashing a quarterback. Maylor let out a gasp. The gun in his hand suddenly went off, the sound of a bullet exploding into a nearby box. David drove Maylor all the way into the concrete. The man's head hit hard on the floor, and the gun bounced from his hand and skidded away from them.

Getting up, David felt a searing pain shoot up his left arm. He thought he might have broken his wrist. His fingers felt like they were on fire. Maylor seemed dazed and dizzy. He tried to push himself up but then slumped back down to the concrete. David looked around but didn't see where the gun had settled. Again, Maylor tried to get up, but David didn't let him. He stepped over and kicked the man straight in the gut as hard as he could. Maylor let out a gasp and collapsed again. David searched the floor but couldn't find the weapon. He needed the gun. He knew Maylor had someone with him. Where was the other guy?

"Mr. Adams?"

David turned, spotted Parker appear from between two crates. The boy wasn't wearing a shirt and looked so frail and scared standing there. He rushed over to the boy, grabbed him by the arm. "We have to get you out of here right now."

David spotted the other guy out of the corner of his eye. He was about thirty feet down the aisle from them, gun already raised in his hand. With his good arm, David immediately pulled Parker behind him just as the guy pulled the trigger. The bullet caught David in the right bicep and sent a second wave of shooting pain through him. The impact made his whole body spin around. But without slowing down, David grabbed Parker, shoved him into another row, and then followed him. Another gunshot rang out. A bullet ricocheted off the metal of the shelves.

David pushed Parker forward, yelling, "Go! Go! Go!"

They both ran as fast as they could up the row, back toward the front entrance to the warehouse. David made sure to run directly behind Parker. If more bullets started flying, he would be sure they hit him first. Not the boy. The opening for the huge garage door was about ten paces ahead of them. They were almost to the outside again. Five more steps. Three. Two. One. David and Parker burst into the parking lot and were immediately blinded by a wave of bright headlights.

Reaching out to Parker, David yanked him to a sudden stop. He was unsure what was happening. Had more of Dyson's guys arrived to go after them? Were they about to be met with more gunfire? David pulled Parker completely behind him. He would die if he could save the kid. David squinted into the glare and braced himself. But he could now hear sirens and see more cars arriving and screeching to a stop all around the front of the building. A group of five or six men was running up to them with their guns drawn.

"Get down! Get down!" one of them was yelling.

David grabbed Parker, pulled him to the ground, wrapped both arms around him, just as the men started firing their weapons. David turned slightly, looked behind him, and watched Richie Maylor and the other guy take direct hits to the chest and shoulders. Both men instantly dropped to the pavement a few feet behind them. David turned his attention to Parker beneath him. Was the boy okay? Was he hurt? Parker had his eyes closed and his arms wrapped around David's waist so tightly, he could barely breathe. David could now hear a helicopter somewhere above him. Several men circled around David and Parker within seconds.

"FBI," one announced. "Are either of you hurt?"

Another FBI agent answered for David, who was too stunned to even speak at the moment. "Get a medic! He's bleeding badly."

David started to get dizzy. In his blurred state, he spotted more police cars arriving on the scene, sirens wailing, lights flashing. It looked like the helicopter was landing in the parking lot just behind them. Two people jumped out of the chopper. David squinted. Zegers? Jess? Was it really them? Or was he beginning to hallucinate?

One of the FBI agents got right in David's face. "Sir, you're going to have to let go of the boy so we can properly care for him."

David looked down, realized he still had a fully flexed arm locked tightly around Parker's midsection. He didn't want to let go. Ever.

FIFTY-TWO

David opened his eyes. He was staring up at a dark sky. For a moment, he wondered if it was all a dream. Had he actually saved Parker? Was the boy really safe? He tried to sit up, realized he was lying on top of a stretcher in the parking lot right in front of the same warehouse where FBI agents had swarmed him. His right arm was completely wrapped in thick white bandages. His left wrist had some kind of brace on it.

"Take it easy, Mr. Adams," said a kind voice to his right.

He turned, noticed an EMT with black spiky hair adjusting some kind of kit that had tubes attached to his wrist. "Where's Parker?"

The EMT looked over at him. "The boy? He's fine. My partner has him up in the ambulance running routine tests. But you don't need to be making any sudden movements. You lost a lot of blood, sir."

"I got shot," David stated, more as if reminding himself of what had just transpired.

The EMT smiled. "Yes, I know that. I've had a good look at it. Fortunately, it was only a flesh wound. No serious damage. On the other hand, I think your wrist is fractured in multiple places. We'll need to get a better look at it when we get you over to the hospital in a moment."

David spotted Parker off to his right, sitting in the back of an ambulance with another female EMT. The boy looked okay. Someone had put a jacket on him. Right next to the boy sat Jess Raven. David hadn't been hallucinating. She was actually there. Jess was holding the boy's hand while the medic searched his eyes with some kind of light. Over to his left, David noticed Harry Zegers speaking with two FBI agents wearing dark windbreakers. There were more agents and police officers all over the place. It felt like a war zone. Zegers turned toward David, noticed he was alert, and then came right over to him.

"Glad to see you up and at 'em again," Zegers said.

"What . . . happened?"

"Jess finally got word to me. We immediately jumped into the chopper to race down here. I'm sorry it took me so long, but it looks like we got here just in the nick of time."

"Is Richie Maylor . . . ?"

"Dead, yes, along with his friend, Manuel Garcia."

"What about Farley?"

Zegers sighed, nodded. "We arrested him. I'm really sorry, David. I guess the man had a gambling addiction I knew nothing about. Left himself vulnerable with a huge debt he couldn't repay. And it almost cost us everything."

"I'm sorry, too. I know you trusted him. What about your son? Is he okay?"

"Yes, he's safe. Dyson is one sick bastard."

"Did you get him?"

Zegers nodded again. "Yeah, we got him. And Christina Legley. That woman cracked almost immediately upon opening the door and finding FBI agents outside. She pinned it all on Dyson. Said he came up with the plan and talked her into going through with it. We'll see what the truth is as we make our way through official interviews."

"So, is it . . . over, Harry?"

"Yes, thanks mainly to you and Jess."

"What about Parker?"

"He's free to go, David."

"You mean that?"

Zegers pressed his lips together. "Hell yeah, I mean it. I owe that boy more than his freedom, but it's the best I can do right now. I just hope Parker can somehow come out of this okay. He's been to hell and back."

"I plan to make sure of that."

Zegers let out a heavy sigh. "Been a helluva day, huh?"

David actually chuckled. "You can say that again."

"How about you and me grab a beer when the dust settles?"

"Yeah, sounds good. But you're paying."

Zegers smiled. "Deal."

Zegers's phone rang, so he picked up the call and wandered off.

Jess slipped in beside David. "Hey, you," she said, placing a warm hand on his bandaged shoulder. "How're you feeling?"

"Better by the moment because of whatever my EMT friend here is starting to pump through this tube."

They shared a grin. Her hand stayed on his shoulder. Jess looked so damn beautiful standing there and staring down at him. Maybe it was the morphine, but he really wanted to pull her in close and kiss her. But he still wasn't sure how she really felt about him. Their entire brief relationship had been a roller-coaster ride of life-and-death emotions and fever-pitched adrenaline. It was difficult for him to tell what was real and wasn't real at the moment. Plus, Jess still seemed to be healing from her husband's tragic death. Although he felt very close to her right now, David wanted to take it slow and be patient.

"Thanks for coming," he said.

"We barely made it."

"But you made it—and that's all that matters."

She sighed, shook her head. "You got yourself shot, David."

"I know," he said with a wide smile. "How about that? Do I get to join your exclusive club now?"

Jess laughed, then scrunched up her mouth. "I don't know. Yours was barely a flesh wound. I'll have to think about it."

"Fair enough." David glanced over toward Parker. "He doing okay?"

She nodded. "Probably the toughest kid I've ever been around."

"Zegers said he's free to go now."

She gave a slight smile. "You really did it, David."

"No, we did it," he clarified. "Seriously, Jess, I couldn't have managed any of this without you. I owe you so much."

She shrugged. "Just fulfilling my judicial responsibility."

"Right. I guess your forty hours are nearly up, huh?"

"Nearly."

"Does that mean you'll be headed back to one of the big firms?"

"I don't know. I'm actually starting to like this gig and my new friends. And I need to help get Bobby Lee back on his feet so he can return to his guard post. So maybe I'll hang around your dust bowl a little longer. See what happens next. If that's okay with you."

She offered him a guarded smile. But the look in her eyes let David know she was hanging around for much more than her new homeless friends.

"I'd like to see what happens next, too, Jess."

Parker was finally brought over to see David. The boy had a few scratches on his forehead and a big bruise on his chin but otherwise looked to be in good shape.

"How're you doing, kiddo?" David asked.

"Better than you, Mr. Adams."

David smiled. "What? This?" He nonchalantly held up his bandaged arm. "This is no big deal. I'll be fine in a few days."

The boy grinned. Then his face drooped. "I'm real sorry I ran again."

"Don't be. I would've run, too, Parker."

The kid noticeably swallowed, stared at the ground. "Do I have to go with the FBI now, Mr. Adams? Will they be putting me into that Witness Protection Program we talked about?"

"Good news, kid. You're done with the FBI."

Parker lifted his head, eyes narrow. "You mean it?"

"I do. This thing is over for you."

Parker's face lit up with relief but then quickly dimmed again.

"What is it?" David asked him.

"I'm glad it's over, Mr. Adams. But . . . where do I go now?"

There was a desperation in the boy's question that immediately made David's eyes well up with tears. But David already knew the answer to that question. He'd been thinking about it from the moment he'd first met Parker. There was something deep in the aching heart of the boy that reached out to him in a way he couldn't explain. He now understood there was a bigger reason why he was the one who'd walked into the juvenile detention center the other night. He knew it the moment he watched Parker run away from him after escaping the ambush downtown. David knew it when he jumped into his truck back in Austin to race down to the border to try to save this precious boy. He knew it when he'd pulled Parker in behind him to shield him from that bullet. Hell, maybe he knew it in his heart from the very first time he set eyes on him. They were meant to be together.

"How about you come stay with me?" David said.

Parker tilted his head. "For real?"

"Yes. I would love to have you with me."

"Okay, that would be *so* cool . . . but for how long, do you think?"

David pulled the boy in close to him. Tears hit his cheeks.

"Forever, Parker. I'm thinking forever."

AUTHOR'S NOTE

For the past fourteen years, I've had the life-changing opportunity to build genuine relationships with so many homeless individuals, including runaway street kids like Parker Barnes, through my work with a nonprofit called Mobile Loaves & Fishes and the Community First! Village—a fifty-one-acre master-planned community in Austin that provides affordable, permanent housing and a supportive community for those coming out of chronic homelessness. I write about these experiences and how they helped inspire the David Adams series on my website at www.chadzunker.com.

ABOUT THE AUTHOR

Chad Zunker is the author of the David Adams legal thriller *An Equal Justice*, which was nominated for the 2020 Harper Lee Prize for Legal Fiction. He also penned its sequel, *An Unequal Defense*, and *The Tracker*, *Shadow Shepherd*, and *Hunt the Lion* in the Sam Callahan series. He studied journalism at the University of Texas, where he was also on the football team. Chad has worked for some of the country's most powerful law firms and has also invented baby products that are sold all over the world. He lives in Austin with his wife, Katie, and their three daughters and is hard at work on his next novel. For more information, visit www.chadzunker.com.